STEVEN

C000004458

BETHANY

CHILLER ®

DREAMING BIG PUBLICATIONS

HEAVEN'S LAMENTABLE LOSS…

HELL'S PROPRIETARY GAIN…

SALVATION IN HER NAME.

THE MOST INTIMATE TALE OF DEMONIC
POSESSION EVER TOLD!

BETHANY

Attention, reader!

The author wishes to note that you will notice he has taken a certain degree of creative license with regards the characters and their origins, in (t)his quasi-religious work of fiction.

There is no offense intended.

SPOILER

Bethany reveals at the start just what it was that the fabled tent held for her in her adolescence.

If you prefer, you can skip right now to that memory at the end of this book before reading her full story.

She'd like that.

And I find more bitter than death the woman, whose heart [is] snares and nets [and] her hands [as] bands, whoso pleaseth God shall escape from her; but the sinner shall be taken by her.

Ecclesiastes 7:26

**31ST OCTOBER
HER DARKEST DAY**

PROLOGUE

THIS is *not* a pleasant story.

It is more of a graphic account of an awful and sensational incident that I experienced a week ago. This won't be some Herculean epic, either. In truth, it's like a lengthy journal entry, and I'll tell only what needs to be told.

My name is Bethany Childs. My mother told me once that she chose the name 'Bethany' because she liked how compassionate it sounded, and how she imagined that by the time I reached womanhood I would be the kind of person to whom others turn in their time of need. I later learned I was given this name by orders from angels, for it had biblical ties, such as Jesus's ascent into Heaven, and Lazarus' resurrection. I have never even read the Bible; it's God's script for us mortal thespians, though, after what I've experienced, we're something more than actors on the world stage.

Before I go any further, I need to make one thing clear: demons and angels exist. I've seen them. Although they're the same type of entity, and while they are like what's been depicted in films and literature over the years, there remains many differences that extend solely beyond their respective appearances. The same can be said about each other's domain; Heaven and Hell are natural opposites, but they are of the same ethereal coin and it's up to those who toss it to find out which does what. To me, heads is heads and tails is tails. It's as obvious as that. Whichever side comes up, you deal with it, and if need be, you run with it. Oh, god, you *run* with it…

My 'coin' was flipped before I was born. Monarchs of Hell

had the liberty of taking this pre-natal toss and likely relished the result when it returned in their favour. Isn't it funny how humanity's fate is wagered in that way? Perhaps not in the actual flipping of a coin but having something powerful and omnipresent decide what route your life should take before you're even down the birth canal–your placenta in tow, sustaining your lifeline–whilst demons busily carve out all kinds of wicked, ungodly mechanisms for your employ. It's not the way for any baby to be brought into the world.

What happened to me–my transformation, the literal demonisation of my former self–is all true. I need you to believe that. There's not a minute that goes by since that awful, terrifying night–which replays in my mind, frighteningly unrestrained–that doesn't make me regret having ever gone to the stupid house party in the first place. I still bear the scars, mentally and physically, inside and out, having been torn in that virginal place I sought hard to protect.

Then there is Amy. Or, that is what the demon calls itself. I don't doubt demons can alter their sex (it *is* the 21st Century), but this Sapphic seducer tethered herself to me almost immediately after my assault, claiming knowledge of it beforehand, then promised revenge and redemption if I chose to be 'christened' by her.

I've already warned you: this isn't a pleasant story. It's *my* nightmare. Revenge is sweet, but it's also dangerous and untamed. I know that now. I broke the rules of Heaven by following the commandments of Hell. If God has looked at what I have done, I hope He can forgive me… even if I feel that nothing on Earth will.

ONE

IN the recesses of my mind, there lies a fragmented memory involving the discovery of a tent which had been tacked down in a sodden field near my Aunt Jennifer's home, round about when I was twelve years old. My cousin and I investigated it one night, believing in the local talk that it was haunted. I've blacked out a lot of this incident that occurred way back then; it serves no purpose in the monstrous creature I have now become; and was only really remembered when Amy spoke of it upon meeting me the night I came home, with my clothes ripped and my make-up smeared.

The finding of the tent was perhaps the main catalyst in all this insanity.

With my heart pounding every step of the way, we fought through stalks of whipping corn whilst ankle-deep in marsh, and swatted nocturnal insects that were out looking to feed and mate, until we reached the clearing where the swamp-green prism had been pitched all on its lonesome. I hesitated; failing to grab my cousin to hold him back, he was too keen to get up close.

I had to get closer, praying that there was no one inside of it. It was around midnight by the time we got there; the moon, if I remember, was disco-balling its radiance through the clouds, through the tree mesh, with shards of light appearing on the ground as if creating a silvery path that led onward. Had the demon, Amy, revealed herself to me then and there, it surely would have been the pinnacle of the supernatural activity that was set in motion to engulf me. And all before I was sixteen. *Sweet sixteen.*

The zip was up; the tent was open! I crept in and found a

torch on the ground sheet. I've since told myself over and over, "*You should* never *have turned on the torch, Bethany!*" and while this "told-you-so" statement is so god-damn redundant now, I can't help but think if maybe I had listened to my instinct that night then I would have saved myself from a fate that was unwinding. Or then again, perhaps I wouldn't have been saved at all.

Inside the tent, there were pornographic magazines scattered everywhere; female flesh scarcely covered by erotic lingerie and sex-catalogue apparel; a carnal library I had the misfortune of looking at. Though I hadn't known exactly what to expect to find inside the tent, this was the last thing I ever imagined I would see. I thought I'd come across a dead body or drugs paraphernalia, neither of which would have done me any good to look at, anyway. But this filth at my early age, whilst not entirely alien to me, didn't pass for regular, homely viewing.

Disgusted, I switched off the torch and threw it aside. When I exited the tent, shaken and sickened, I berated my cousin for dragging us out to the sordid thing, but later realised that I had only been angry at myself for allowing our excursion to happen in the first place. Earlier that day, I had tried to convince him not to go out there. Yet, it was my own curiosity that had got the better of me; I wanted to know what this tent was all about. Anything could have happened to the pair of us—to either of us.

So, what has that got to do with what happened to me years later? I told you that the tent may have been the catalyst that awoke Amy. My own childlike mind: unable to comprehend and make sense of the events of that night and disturbing the sleeping demon, rousing her to take charge of matters on earth.

Wait a minute—I never properly introduced myself, did I? For all my sixteen years, I was known as Bethany Childs. After my rape, my demonic christening transpired, and I became Amy's 'property', a prisoner in her infernal custody: *Bethany Chiller*. My sole purpose: to wreak havoc on my attackers, to avenge my stolen innocence; to feature, in a way, in a tale like Job's; by having a subordinate of Hell affect my decisions and test my reverence before God, who surely would not have let this young girl suffer *so badly* to begin with…

TWO

THERE is absolutely nothing special about the rural town that I live in, save for its background as a proud, Scottish mining settlement. Its placement between two famous cities is satirical: each city being a cheek on the derriere of the body-map that's Scotland. There are no ancient Celtic burial grounds from where the dead will rise; no shops or private stores of antiquity opening with artefacts everyone desires. In fact, about a year before, after the area was upgraded to town status, it began to feel like a ghost town. Shops started closing at the drop of a hat, it seemed, and the lacklustre response from inept councillors and political candidates was that all good things eventually happen in time. It's a customary response from the white-collar establishment. Happy to let things simmer and see what comes of it.

My darkest day began on the thirty-first of October. It was also the day of my sixteenth birthday.

There was nothing instinctual surrounding me when I awoke; nothing to announce that in the next twelve hours, I would see the world in a whole new light (or darkness, take your pick). I awoke up with the hope my bust size had increased, like Molly Ringwald in the movie *Sixteen Candles*. I had been standing in front of the mirror that was screwed to the back of my bedroom door, and I was taking in what was meant to be a magical, private moment in my young life. But the reflection relayed the same visual message that it had done the day before–and had done the past 365 before that–deflating my expectations of what my body should have morphed into overnight. I looked on hurtfully in the mirror, ponderingly, for it was to be my last eight hours of uninterrupted sleep as an all-human girl, and the only thing that bugged me then was that my breasts were still a 30A. I kept on checking, however; twisting this way and that, looking for the smallest, inflated improvement. In the end, I had to pretend that I had 'ballooned', praying it would make me feel better for the rest of the day. I remember blowing an exaggerated kiss into that mirror, thinking, *Samantha Baker, this one's for you!*

It did occur to me to consider taking the day off. It was my sixteenth: the all-important, coming-of-age birthday that meant the world to my mother, to me, and to my best friend, Michelle. In hindsight–that glorious, belated perception!–I should have stayed home. Then, I'd never have known about the house party, or encountered the four masked skeletons who brutalised me. Though, as I now am aware, Amy had been anticipating the attack. Creatures in Hell love rolling dice, I hear. It's even better when they're loaded. What is it they say? The house always wins?

There was another reason why I couldn't stay home: I had volunteered that year to help with the preparation for the school's Halloween party. The other pupils, particularly the younger ones, required in-depth direction to set up the horror theme: entry tickets, food and drink, music, contest judging and prize giveaway-arranging. While I wasn't the only hardworking pupil on the 5th Year committee, I did feel like it was my duty to spearhead the party planning: one last major event before I was due to leave for college after the summer.

My tabby cat was curled up on my bed as if it were her very own. Through marble-green eyes, she eyed me as I pouted and posed in front of the mirror. Then, she yawned, as if bored, and slowly stretched out her limbs. The cat yawning somehow made me think of the lions on the Serengeti plains; jaws with teeth so ferocious and scary that it could put you off visiting parts of eastern Africa. Even though my cat was a fraction of the size of those beasts, utilising the power I have now it would not seem surreal to me if a lioness had been laying there.

"You're awake now?" I said to the cat. "Well, what do you think? I'm another year older. Does it show? Do *these* look any bigger?"

My cat doesn't lie, but it rarely tells the truth. I could have awoken with implanted DDs and the lazy feline would still have lain there, viewing me with a look so startlingly casual and simple that even under the weight of my new implants I would feel the disparagement.

"You're not sure, either, are you? Well, wish me 'happy birthday' whenever you feel like it!"

The cat yawned again, without sound, without a care, and re-curled on the bed.

I left for the bathroom to get ready for school. Genetic traits ensured I had my mother's long black hair and model face (I'm not vain; I'm just honest!)–features which had been horribly contorted on the night of my attack.

I showered and returned to my room, spraying myself with my favourite Impulse deodorant, vaporising the room with its sweet scent. I kept things girly where I could.

In the corner, there was a wicker chair, one of the few personal items left after my father died. Seated there, was my Halloween outfit: a zombie cheerleader, complete with proper, black and red pom-poms. The dress colour was blood-red with black frilly trimming; its pre-torn hem flirted above the knee. My friend, Michelle, noted the skin visible from the bottom of my dress to the top of my knee-high socks (she actually thought there wasn't enough on show!). The blonde woman on the cover looked overtly sexual, with her hands high in the air, shaking the pom-poms excitedly, her legs crossed at that desirable-intersection where her slim, netted thighs met. Oh, and there was the wink from one smoky eye, which made me wonder why on earth anyone would fall for her ocular gesture when she planned on having them for dinner.

I finished dressing into jeans and a school-branded jumper. I always left the bedroom door open for the cat to get in and out. As I left the room to go downstairs, I could hear music coming from the kitchen. I knew it was from the kitchen because that's where my mother had placed the DAB radio that she bought on sale from Argos. She hadn't figured out how to operate it fully yet, so we would have anything from pop to rock music at any mealtime. It was quite welcoming that her music taste was ostensibly varied!

"Good morning, Bethany!" my mother called.

I entered the kitchen to a panorama of pink balloons, twisting, dangling streamers, and foil letters and numbers tacked to the wall that celebrated: HAPPY 16TH BETHANY. It looked like an explosion of shining pink and metallic silver– I wouldn't have liked it any other way. I wished that Samantha Baker had awoken to something like this instead.

I walked over to hug my mother; the embrace summed up the last few years in its clinch. With my dad gone–having died three years before–my mother had taken on the challenge of dual parenting with fiery optimism. This date today, a threshold had been crossed, that challenge faced and stared down. It was just the two of us from then, and it remained the two of us now.

"My big girl!" my mother said, holding back tears. "A woman now! Oh, it's all moving so fast!"

I pulled away, a little embarrassed. Had I known half of the intricate stuff that I know now, I wouldn't have been so easily discomfited.

"Mum! Come on, you'll crush my jumper!"

"I'm sorry, honey. Sixteen today–of *all* days!"

"Well, you did have all those years to prepare for it!" I berated her, playfully.

"I've *always* hated your birthday being on Halloween! Your dad never minded. In fact, he used to joke about it."

I rummaged in the fridge for a carton of fresh orange juice. I found it and took a glass from an overhead cupboard. It was important for me to keep up the vitamins.

"Can't do much about that," I said, sitting by the breakfast bar. "I'm my own woman now. It's hard to take in, still, that he's not with us anymore to see."

"I know. But he wouldn't have wanted to see you upset on your birthday. Hey, do you like the decorations? They're not a bit much, are they?"

"Course not, mum. They're lovely. Pink is just so… me!" I

replied.

"You want anything for breakfast before I leave for work?"

"No, I'm good. I'll grab something when I get to school. I'll still catch the breakfast club if I leave in five."

My mother was full of energy this morning. She once told me about a dream that she had that was like a movie-like replay of when she had given birth to me, pushing me out into the world in a gushing pool of water, blood and excrement (I don't know why I needed to know all that!). No woman ever forgot *that* experience, and no man–no matter how comparably he matched the pain, be it kicked in the balls or a left-right combo by a young, hungry Mike Tyson–could ever experience it. Perhaps sure enough, many women wished that their male partners could feel the piercing agony of childbirth, but it was a gift, a sensation–a great-fucking-sensation!–from the Lord, courtesy of Eve's folly.

"I don't know if I'll be home by dinner, but I'll try. We've got a lot of long evening meetings coming up since they announced the company merger. Are you all set for tonight?"

"Yes: we've got the school disco to set up and close, then I'm off to Michelle's for the night. And, you don't need to explain, mum. I know you've got to work."

"Michelle…?"

"Mum, we talked about this," I groaned. We were, again, shaking the pillars of an argument that had been building in recent months.

"Honey, I'm not sure Michelle's such a good…" Her sentence didn't need to be finished for me to know what she was trying to say.

"Mum, Michelle's been my friend for as long as I can remember," I found myself stating. "We do everything together. You know that."

My mother came and stood by me, draping her arm over my shoulder. She squeezed tightly.

"I'm only saying, Bethany. That hassle last year with the pregnancy…"

"Mum!"

My mother turned and walked away, her hands raised as if she had said something remarkably offensive and was attempting to disclaim it. In a way she had, and we both knew it. She had mentioned something that both Michelle and I vowed to never speak of again. There was a darkness in each of our teenage lives that both of us wanted kept from the light.

"I'm sorry, Bethany," my mother said. "You know I'm just looking out for you."

I cooled a little. I was close to finishing my orange juice. Sitting prim on the stool, I allowed myself to relax a bit more. It was *my* day. Besides, my mother was right: she was only looking out for me. The pregnancy matter with Michelle had been a dire episode in our lives. Each of us was content to store it away deep in our memory, under a mental lock and key. Though sometimes, Michelle said things that made me wonder if the situation surfaced within her more often than she let on. It wasn't just a pregnancy scare that had rocked our underage world–the subsequent abortion had, too.

"It's not your fault, mum," I said, rather hushed as I broke off from my thoughts. "We don't talk about what happened to Michelle. That's all in the past."

"Just the other day you said–"

"The other day was a year ago in my life, mum. Let's leave it back there, okay?"

A silence fell over us for the next minute. My mother finished up and left the kitchen. I lowered my head, blew out my cheeks; I was afraid that I had upset her with my no-nonsense choice of words. I decided to let the matter slip, go find my mother, and clear it up.

The two of us eventually met in the hallway; I was putting on my coat to leave for school.

"Have you got everything?" my mother asked.

"For what I need in the world? I should have–you gave me it all, mum."

That made my mother smile, my unwavering charm and discerning approach to life. I needed no lessons on how to be respectful and considerate. They were priceless, affectionate comportments that, if installed at birth, would be simpler to manage later in life.

"I'm afraid you're going to need a lot more than what you've got before you take on what's out there, young lady!"

We stood one in front of the other; my mother helped button me up, as she had done for fifteen years at various ages and stages, whether it was warranted or not.

"I think I can get the last one!"

My mother stopped. There were tears in her eyes as she looked at me. She cherished moments like this, from the first days at primary school; when dressing me up in costumes for dances or recitals or family gatherings; when picking me up and cleaning my wounds or wiping away tears. Her baby girl had grown up. If only she knew what I was bound to become.

"Have a great day, today," she said to me, before kissing me on the forehead. "Your dad would be so proud. If he's watching over us, I know there'll be a celebration in Heaven. He'll have all the angels dancing for you!"

"I know he will."

I turned; *This is it*, I thought optimistically, as I pulled open the front door. *Time to get out there and become part of the 'adult' world!*

THREE

I stepped out to view the dull, Scottish landscape; rain during the night had slickened the streets. It was damp, and it was grey and unwelcoming. The sun, ever shielded by lacklustre clouds, perched high above the earth.

"Happy birthday, *you!*"

I reached the end of the path, to the garden gate, when I heard her. My friend, Michelle, was making her way up from her own home, which was some houses down. She was smiling despite the chilly air and waving a small box that was wrapped in coloured paper for me to take notice. It was like a joke about the French waving a white flag at the start of war; desperate to be observed, to be *spared*.

"See?" said Michelle as she approached the gate where I stood. "I told you *I* wouldn't forget!"

I left the familiarity of the garden path, that concrete trail I had come to know entirely in all my sixteen years, from bouncing to skipping to running along its slabbed surface, chasing after friends and ice-cream vans.

"I didn't think you would," I returned, sincerely.

We were face to face moments later; Michelle hugged me tight—so tight it might have been mistakenly viewed as being something sensual. We could have been a mortal representation of that Taoist symbol, yin and yang (me with my smooth, raven hair; Michelle with her curled, milk-white tassels), but strictly in appearance only. Each of us preserved our own unique duality.

Michelle handed over the wrapped item; both her hands went into mine, as if she was passing over a defrayal, a critical, one-of-a-kind gift that could serve to lift or worsen worldly tribulations. I accepted it thus, it being something from a lifelong friend.

"What is it?" I asked, lightly shaking the box.

"Open it and see, silly!" she said.

I wasted no time in tearing open the wrapper. There was a wine-red jewellery box inside. I cupped it carefully, before prising open the lid to reveal a gold-plated, halved heart pendant on a thin necklace.

"I have the other half," Michelle said. She unbuttoned the top of her blouse and gently pulled her necklace out. "It's from my sixteenth. I hid this from you because I wanted you to have this half. It was my surprise."

I pulled the pendant free from its secure position in the box. It was a light piece of jewellery on an even lighter, gold chain. Michelle came closer and pressed her gold half against mine; it made a beautiful whole pieced together.

"I love it," I told her, truthfully, admiring the paired heart, then, looking into her blue eyes.

She hugged me again; I felt her breasts press against mine. Hers were bigger, heavier, which I envied. Thinking back, there was so much warmth radiating from her that morning.

"Now, come on," Michelle said, dropping her necklace back into her blouse. "We'd better get to school. P.E. today! We don't want Dickson moaning at us for being late again!"

"It's only because you want him to see you in the showers!" I teased, placing my new birthday gift in my coat pocket.

"Hey!" she snapped back. "Besides, it's not only me!"

We walked together down the road. If we'd been any closer, we might as well have been holding hands.

Unknown to us at that time, we *were* being watched. Thanks to the demonic power I possess, I was granted full knowledge of everything that happened in that week. Here's a little side-track to my story that's just as disgusting and perverted as what transpired that Halloween night.

*****

There is a house across the street, which is nothing unusual as there's a line of them that runs each way and is what makes our street. Some are good-looking sturdy new-builds while others are run-down council- or tenant-owned properties. The adults, including my mother, suspected that there was someone living in that one house across from us who had a predatory past. As in, a fetish for young girls.

They say talk is cheap, but the rumours hanging around this individual were big money words.

His name was Graeme and he was an ex-postman. The story was that he had become infatuated with a young mother in a different area (likely where he had worked his delivery route) and, after striking up a friendly relationship with her, began seeing her outside of his working hours. Nothing wrong with that, right? It gets murky.

He wasn't a looker, not the Gerard Butler type of Scotsman that you would die to find on a hot summer's day on an Ayrshire seafront; the girl enjoyed that he had money from his post office shares and regular wage, and so for a while they were inseparable. He took her out to nice restaurants; on days out with her and her daughter. You may be thinking that there's nothing wrong with that and many would agree with you. You're probably right.

He was only approaching forty…

She had only left the last of her teenage years behind.

But it wasn't *her* he was interested in…

I don't want to drag you any farther into the fold; many corrupted souls linger on the cusp of such degrading conduct, hoping to lap up any spoiled dregs that the living may have cluttered around their own existence. This bastard could have destroyed a young family unit–albeit incomplete–with his disturbing fascination for pre-schoolers. Luckily for the mother, who almost always never left him alone with her child, she spotted his twisted proclivities by accidentally stumbling across images on his mobile phone. Thankfully for her, they weren't of any youngsters she knew–certainly not any of her own daughter–but they were other people's children.

Children.

That was over a year ago. He somehow found his way onto our street, and the talk soon began.

He began watching Michelle and I not long after he moved in. My unearthly acuity revealed everything I didn't really want to know. Like, he often watched us from a window at the top of his house; that nasty, curtain-twitcher, hungrily peeking out of the side as we teenage girls went about our business. Pulling aside the curtain with one grubby little hand whilst the other pulled at his grubby little-

Michelle had heard the rumours too, from her own parents' talk. And seeing as no crime had ever been committed (other than the photos he possessed, which resulted in him losing his job and being rehoused after being 'victimised') there wasn't much anyone could do, neither the police nor neighbourhood watch. Everyone was resigned to keeping an eye out whenever Graeme came out.

So, with the help of Amy's intervention, I found I could 'see' into people's lives: what they did, how they did it, with whom and where. It was a psychic connection that I had full control of, with a touch of clairvoyance and telekinesis thrown in for good measure. It enabled me to touch people in more ways than one. For instance, I could castrate a man without holding a knife just by merely willing it, if I knew he had attacked an innocent woman. My powers could allow me to view the horrific act he had committed, before the telekinesis enabled me to interfere with the physical world, causing objects to move or be thrown, or to be sliced and slashed—all at my whim. With demons like Amy coming to the rescue of tortured maidens like me, it truly could be a girl's world.

Graeme, forty-years old with an enervating heart-condition, one solitary criminal conviction, and employment contract termination to his name, kept printed photos of us on his bedroom wall. Of course, they were of a non-sexual nature to the normal eye, but to someone like him they were pornographic material that he could hunch over and whip himself into a frenzy whilst icing his fingers with his gunk.

Yes, I knew he had done this. Several times.

I was forced to deal with Graeme after I disposed of two of my rapists. Though I didn't set out to kill him—he ended up that way because I chose not to turn the other cheek. I stopped being that person early on that week in my life. More on that later. I did say he was only a side-track to my story.

FOUR

WE made it to the school in time. Just as we entered the main building, the sky cracked open and it rained and thundered hard like nothing before. It was torrential.

Inside the foyer, I could see that some of the party decorating had already begun. There was a banner hanging there, with orange and black streamers at either end, dangling just above head height. Paintings of pumpkins adorned the banners, and actual carved pumpkins, with grinning faces yet to be lit, were on tables in rows. We were using battery-operated candles this year. The school didn't want to risk fires using real candles. We had used some of the school funds to purchase an insane amount of those battery-powered candles from Poundland.

I'll always remember it being a good high school. It's now impossible for me to return at this time, being what I am, but I can still know how things are going there. After my attack and subsequent revenge–including the bonfire–something stirred within the pupils and staff. Whilst some pupils introverted, becoming less keen on speaking about things that had happened to them in their own lives, others opened up more and stepped out in search of their own answers. I only wish for the sake of those unable to help themselves, that I could whisper to them that Heaven *is* watching, that they are under God's watchful eye, and to be careful about the choices they make now and in the future. It's kind of unfair how our decision-making is used like that, but it is how we're judged in the end, I guess. We're all the same. Well, some of us, anyway. I'm likely the exception.

Michelle and I had the same P.E. class on our timetable. It was every Monday morning. We had up to ten minutes in the changing rooms to get ready.

Today's class was volleyball. An activity that featured a hall half-full of teenage girls bouncing up and down swatting balls over a net. No wonder the boys liked to watch from the sides.

I was sitting alone in the empty locker-room; echoes of activity sounded around me, but it was otherwise quiet where I was. I slipped out of my jeans and jumper and pulled my sportswear from my locker. I stood in my pants and T-shirt, shivering a little due to the cool air that circulated in the locker-room, before pulling on my shorts. They were tight around my waist. I ponytailed my long hair and slid into my shoes, the kind with the magic sole that didn't mark the linoleum when your feet braked hard.

"Bethany…"

I had heard my name being whispered, as if carried among the echoes; but also as if it was spoken by someone behind me. Undeterred, despite being one-hundred percent sure I had heard it, I ignored it and stuffed my belongings in the locker. I turned the lock and wrapped the key on the rubber band around my wrist. It caught my skin as I stretched it over my hand.

"Bethany…"

Someone had called out to me again; it was a louder attempt and this time I did turn to face the doorway, where I expected someone to be standing there berating me for taking my time. But, as you'll have guessed, there was nobody there.

"I'll be there in a minute," I shouted back anyway, in case someone *was* outside in the hallway shouting at me from afar. Though, I hadn't seen any of the other girls nearby. I usually was the last to get ready.

I felt a hand grip my shoulder. I spun quickly, fright stripping me inside out. It was only Michelle. She jumped, too, startled.

"Hey!" I shouted.

"Sorry, Bethany," she said, sincerely. "I just wondered where you were. You've been ages."

It took me a few moments to calm down. I laughed, feeling

stupid. I saw that Michelle was holding one of the balls from the gymnasium.

"It's okay, I'm just a bit jumpy. Halloween and all that."

"You should be used to it by now," Michelle said. "It's *your* big day today! You should be out there on the court."

"You're right," I agreed. "Let's go and show them how to do it!"

Michelle turned; she was a beautiful specimen in that light, that shape. Her shorts were shorter and tighter than mine, revealing full, thick thighs any lover would kill to get their hands on. And her hair; blonde and tied back, like mine, with a high ponytail.

"Well?" she said, passing the ball from one hand to the other. "Are you ready to bash some balls?"

I broke away from admiring her beauty to take in her indecorous remark.

"Huh?"

Michelle dragged me out of the girls' locker-room, as I clung onto her, laughing my backside off. I didn't mention to her that I had heard someone calling me; at the time, in fact, I think I forgot it had even happened, but then…

I hadn't known the sound of Amy's voice.

FIVE

AN hour later, a classful of sweaty, chirpy teen girls spilled into the changing room. Above the noise of their chatter and the opening and slamming of locker doors, our P.E. teacher shouted to us as he passed the doorway that we did good. Although he may have said some edgy things in the time I knew him, I know for certain that he was not a pervert or deviant. Again, it's down to that supernatural thing I possess.

"I can't believe we won again!" Michelle exclaimed. "This gets easier every week!"

"Yeah," I backed her up. I was close to finish getting dressed. "Maybe soon we'll get some real competition?"

I closed my locker door and leaned closer to Michelle. "You've got to stop teasing old Dickson! Poor guy's going to have a heart attack the next time you bend over like that while stretching!"

"Oh?" she replied. "And what about you? Running and jumping without your sports-bra on! You *better* remember to bring it next week! And, you need to take good care of your hamstrings, Bethany."

I blushed. She had me there. It hadn't been intentional. I had forgotten my sports-bra, which didn't make it easy when you were jumping to hit the ball over the net. Luckily for me, I wasn't as top-heavy as Michelle, so I wasn't running the risk of black eyes every time I leapt. It wasn't like we were playing Olympic rules, anyway. The games were incredibly basic. Like our skill level.

Before we left the changing room, one of the other girls came over to us. I had known this girl for a while, but we weren't friends. She was the kind you would say hello to if you passed her in the corridor, but then you would worry that they were talking about you later in the day. She hung around with a group of others who acted as idiotic and pompous as anything straight out of a mid-'80s John Hughes movie.

"There's a party tonight at Cameron Davidson's," the girl–Lisa–told me. I tried to take no notice, but Michelle had clocked onto us and was staring.

"Oh, right," I murmured.

"Well, you can come along if you want. I hear it's your birthday, so that's why I'm inviting you." She then looked Michelle up and down with disfavour that hardly went unnoticed by Michelle. "You can come too, I suppose. But, Michelle: try not to make it as dramatic as last year's, okay?"

Michelle slammed her locker door shut, fuming.

"I don't think I could handle another abortion talk in sex ed," Lisa said, smartly, before trotting off back to her stable of friends.

I leaned back against the locker, shocked. Michelle was standing glassy-eyed, looking at Lisa whilst the smug bitch chatted to her clique.

"She is a fucking bitch, Bethany!" Michelle cursed.

"Don't worry about Lisa," I said. "She *is* a bitch! Listen, we don't have to go there tonight."

Michelle looked at me. I could see she was hurting. I could tell even then, without the demonic power.

"No, we'll go," she said, determinedly. "And we'll show them."

I rocked back gently, casually, against the locker. "Whatever you want. But, we're in this together. It's *our* night."

We soon left the locker-room and found we were the only two girls present in the school corridor. Unusual, but you take what peace you can get when it's like this.

Michelle turned to me. "Hey, Bethany, about what Lisa said in there…"

"Didn't I say not to worry? We don't have to go if it bothers you."

"It's not that," Michelle said. She sounded wounded. "What

she said about the talk in class, you know, about the abortion…"

I didn't know how to respond. What was about to happen to me mere hours later had kind of already happened to Michelle one year prior. Though she had consented to the sex when she fell pregnant, as a result it threw the one-off lovers into a mess they weren't prepared for. *He* wanted nothing to do with her afterwards and Michelle, afraid as any fifteen-year old could be in her situation, decided on going alone quietly to the doctor to discuss a termination.

"That's all in the past," I said to her. I rubbed her arm comfortingly. "I know it's hard, but let it go. Leave it there."

"Easier said than done, though," Michelle replied, and I knew that to be true. She looked away from me when she spoke because she knew that I would see her begin to cry.

It was time for us to split up. We hugged before parting for our classes. I would split up from Michelle one more time before the end of my birthday, and it would be the last ever moment I would feel anything remotely human for her.

*****

In among the decorating, the painting, the creating, the fighting, the fussing, the shouting, the preparing, there was a cracking Halloween party being put together. We had the best spooky music set up on a combination of CDs: Ray Parker Jr.'s *Ghostbusters* to Mike Oldfield's *Tubular Bells* theme from *The Exorcist*, we had it all covered. Even *Rocky Horror* made it into the mix–why the hell wouldn't it? These tunes defined modern Halloween parties! *If you could just jump to the left…*

My hours in that day became a memory-mash of orange colours, black cats and hats, grinning pumpkins, and fake candle-flame; it felt like I was running crazy figure-eights from one end of the gymnasium to the other. Only earlier in that day we had been running about, playing volleyball in there; now, it was being rearranged into our forthcoming disco, with tables and banners and streamers of all sorts laid out.

Once we had everything completed satisfactorily, we stood

back and breathed in a heavy intake of anticipation and expectation, before exhaling to relay our nerves in abundance. It was more important than ever for me to see that the event ran smoothly and trouble-free. It enabled me to underline that I had initiative; could organise party events without any issues preceding them. Everything we ordered was locked, stocked, and good to go.

After I praised and thanked everyone for their efforts, I left the school in a hurry. It was only 2 P.M. I then realised I'd forgotten my jacket. Cursing, I turned and headed back up the steps and in through the main doors.

The principal, Mr. Wiseman, was crossing the corridor from one room to his office.

"Bethany?" he called.

I turned to see him standing there. There was nothing wrong or unusual about the guy; a lot of the younger pupils, not knowing any better, made fun of him regularly. I suppose at one time we've all done it. It isn't until you actually stop and speak to them that you realise just what they are doing for our education and our lives. The sacrifices they make, the hours they have to eat up, and when one of them dies, the upset it causes an entire school. We only ever had one teacher who had been killed, which was when he was on a trip abroad during the summer holidays two years back, with his fiancé. We then spent the remainder of that August getting counselling and bereavement support from external, specially-trained staff. At the time, I didn't know what had happened, the ins and outs; but when I came to power this week, I knew his fall had been accidental, his death ugly but instant (I had concentrated on a psychic scan of the entire faculty, same as I'd done with Dickson in P.E.).

Mr. Wiseman had spotted me returning to the school. I guess he was simply curious to know what I was doing wandering in the main hallway.

"Are you alright, Bethany?" he asked. "Is everything ready for this evening?"

"Yes, sir," I said, walking over to him. "We're all set up for the party. If there's anything we missed–and there shouldn't be anything–some of us are arriving earlier anyway just to ensure that we're max-good to go."

He smiled at me as I gave him a thumbs-up.

"We can always rely on you, Bethany," he said. "I've always got time for students like you. You'll go far, I know. Are you still considering going to college?"

"After the summer, sir," I replied, eager to end the conversation so I could get to my jacket. My birthday heart was still in the pocket. "I've got to go just now, sir, but I'll be back for the party."

I quickly returned to the gym-hall. There was no one present while I searched the backs of chairs and on tabletops. I found my jacket under a pile of black cardboard cut-outs of witches and goblins, and bizarre-looking creatures that I took to be ghouls or demons. The creativity here never failed to amaze me! If Dante was alive now, he'd surely have some inspiration to draw from.

I slipped my jacket on, suddenly aware that I was the only one standing in the great big, orange- and black-themed hall. The tables for this evening's party were organised in a horseshoe pattern, freeing up the centre space for the dancing and games that were planned. Looking at it now, in this eerie silence, it felt so open and void. I think at that moment, I shivered. Sure, it was cold outside; November was knocking at every door like a persistent salesman; on every outside surface it could find, but this cold was different. It was situated in that spot right beside me, but I found as I moved to leave it seemed to follow me; a breezy aura, invisibly attached, blowing its wintry breath…

Like something was in the gym-hall with me, watching.

Waiting.

SIX

THERE are two moments I remember most vividly, most horribly, about that Halloween night: one that shook me to the core and another that made me dig right deep into it. It was my reflection before I left the house, and my reflection when I returned in the early hours of that morning, soaked by sweat and rain, and torn and demonically *changed*.

It was going on 3 P.M. by the time I got in the door. My mother was still at work, so I had the house to myself. The kitchen remained as pink and silver as it did that morning, and it moved me to see that it had been left that way. I kicked some balloons as I walked around the house, completely ensuring no-one else was present, before heading upstairs to begin my first transformation: a zombie cheerleader!

I showered, using tons of coconut body wash and Pantene 2-in-1 in my hair. I headed to my room, covered by my towel, and began the protracted process of applying my make-up and brushing out my hair. All the while my costume remained in the wicker chair; out of its packaging, its fabric soaking in the perfumes and smells that radiated around my room so that every inch of it was *me*.

I sat on a stool by the dresser, which had a mirror my height in front. I could ably see my whole upper body reflection; I felt like Whigfield–that forgotten Danish singer–as I propped myself up with just the towel wrapped around me and my hairbrush like a microphone in my hand. There would be no *Saturday Night* singing going on–it was time to soak in the atmospherics of the Pagan rooted-inspired festival and get to work.

I took my time because that's what we girls do when we're

getting dressed up, right? Sure, it wasn't for a date or anything, but I wanted my look to be pretty and practical, so I could be wholly comfortable in something that only came around once a year. I slowly brushed my long black hair straight out, unsure whether to go for the traditional cheerleader-style of hair– 'pigtails', in case you didn't know–or one single high 'ponytail' that spilled from the top and down over my shoulders. My hair was certainly long enough for either style.

I chose the pigtails. They were my favourite, then.

Next thing was to dress up. Though I didn't quite view it as such, it did feel at the time awkwardly *sexual* to be getting into something that showed an awful lot. I suppose the beaming blonde-haired woman on the packaging gave the game away– while her face suggested she enjoyed the attention even more. Pulling up my black and red knee-high socks over my slim, smooth legs should not have made me think of *Lolita*, nor when I stepped into the short, blood-red dress with the black frilly trimming that tickled the front of my bare thighs should I have thought of that same literature again. The lettering on the dress top was the number 69, with my customised initials after it. There were no implications at all–it was just a number, albeit suggestive, chosen by Michelle and me to make the plain white top stand out and appear fancier. I later got the impression it was like sending out the Bat-Signal on a black night in Gotham.

I did feel exposed, self-conscious, but not in danger. That came later.

I wore a pair of canvas shoes so that they were comfortable to wear all evening. I had thought about wearing those secretary-like black patent heels, but they were too tall and racy for me. The canvas shoes felt much better, much softer, to walk in. The website I had visited just happened to have a black pair with red laces. So far, everything in my life at sixteen was going well.

I finished off this pre-evening ritual by completing my makeup. I was inspired by the woman on the cheerleader outfit packaging: I went with the smoky-eyes look. With some foundation brushed in and concealer added, plus a touch of dark red lipstick, I finally finished the look I had envisioned for so long. In the mirror, I sure was a beauty. I looked good, happy, unabridged. In just a matter of hours, this façade would be extinguished forever, and my entire world turned upside down.

It had left 6 P.M. The house remained silent; the DAB radio was off, and my mother still wasn't home. Even as I knew everything was fine and running according to plan, I couldn't shake off that persistent feeling that had been tapping its ice-tipped fingers along my spine. Something about that evening kept nagging me. I put it down to the 'birthday blues'–that I had crossed a threshold into another 'world' (the adult world); perhaps I had got older too quickly, too soon, of which there was nothing I could do about it. Each time I looked into the mirror and saw the horror reflection of myself, I would try to brush aside that haunting feeling. But, like it had been in the school hall, I felt like there was some*thing* else in the room with me, watching me dress, watching me apply cosmetics that in time would make me stand out from a crowd, to be selected by an unknown predatory bunch as their plaything. Amy may have been on the outskirts of this earthly plane I had a stake in, but now she was closer than ever to breaking through and joining me.

She just needed my assault as her summons.

Before I finally left the sanctity of my room, my tabby cat, that mute. mini lioness, remained on my bed, watching me as she had done hours before.

"What do you think now?" I asked it. No reply. "God forbid I ever go out on a date–is that what you're thinking? Are you *that* judgemental?"

Then, I remembered: I hadn't removed the gold half-heart from my jacket pocket. I found it and with both ends of the chain held, I secured it round my neck. In the light from my room the half-heart sparkled upon my chest, just above my small breasts. It looked gorgeous placed there. I felt powerful, like *Wonder Woman*, if she'd been an athletic zombie! I gathered up my pom-poms before leaving the room.

The dark outside was my cloak as I left the house before 7 P.M. I ensured the front door was locked (making note of the spare key hidden in a plant pot, of all places) and I walked down the garden path. Déjà vu set in as I thought of this morning. I could see one or two groups of little horror bodies running from house to house, singing their songs for tricks or treats. Where I lived, they usually got a pound coin. It helped shut them up.

Michelle, again like this morning, was making her way up to me. I could hear her heels clicking on the pavement.

"Gimme a *B!* Gimme a *C!*" she mimicked in the street, throwing around invisible pom-poms in her routine.

When she appeared, she walked into—and was illuminated by—the sodium glow of the streetlight outside of my gate (kind of like Father Merrin outside that infamous, '70s Georgetown house), and I could see how stunning and vibrant and beautiful she looked. *She* was more like the blonde woman from the packaging of my outfit: bubbly and coy. Standing there in that light, she looked considerably older than her years, from her curvilinear shape right down to her confidence and personality. What wasn't there to admire? I look back on moments like this, and I like that feeling I had when I was all human.

She was dressed as a sexy vampire, or some kind of Gothic goddess—either character bled sex appeal. Perhaps more like the Mistress of the Dark, Elvira, aided by the added push-up bra, pale, ghost-white complexion, and bouffant blonde hairdo (the hair colour of the two being the noticeable difference). Her eyes, ringed with a wealth of mascara and eyeshadow, were seductive and appealing.

Her full vertical torso was bookended above her hips by a revealing lace top. It wasn't until she took a small step further that I noticed she had two giant black wings fitted, as well as sleeved, black satin fingerless gloves.

"And what are you supposed to be?" I asked.

"The Angel of *Death!*" she hissed, rainbowing each

upstretched arm in the air. "Failing that, I'll settle for a female Satan. Or, vampire. Which is best? Or worse?"

I didn't like multiple choice questions.

"A *female* Satan? God, that's a new one!" I blasphemed (trust me, I did).

"Well, I prefer the *Black Angel*," she said, delighted, and certain of her choice.

"That sounds like a Marvel character," I teased. "Think you can fly with *those* things?"

I softly pulled at one of her giant black wings. It was surprisingly sturdy and thick.

"Let me think some 'happy thoughts'," Michelle whispered, "and we'll see how high I can fly!"

I closed my gate and we started down the street.

"I really love your costume," I told her. She was a couple of inches taller due to the heels she wore.

"Yours is pretty cool, too," she said, truthfully. She had, after all, helped me pick it out. "I like what you did with the fake blood and scars. The poms are good, too. Will you be eating any *brains* this evening?"

I laughed out loud. My pom-poms were in one hand. I felt them rustling against my thigh as I walked.

"I don't think there are any in our school worth eating!"

"Well, then, eat mine!"

She lowered her head so that she could pretend I was eating into the top of her skull. I could smell the hairspray she had used, an aroma that Medusa herself might have worn before snakes became her once-beautiful locks. It sailed into my nostrils like ships setting forth on an adventurous voyage—determined to make an entrance and an exit.

She had stooped low due to her heels, but when she raised her head, she did so slowly.

"You're wearing your heart," she said, as if she were both shocked and amazed, trailing her gaze from my chest to my eyes, and back.

"Of course I am," I replied. "It's the most beautiful thing I got today. My mum's still waiting on stuff coming, but…"

Michelle then leaned forward, downward, and took me in her gloved arms. I felt the smooth skin of her neck as it slipped off my cheek and lay against mine; the bulge of each pressing breast as she leaned; and again, her fragrance drowned me, preceding her as if she had been an all-powerful Amazonian queen.

"Hey" I gasped, off-guard. "What's that for?"

She peeled away from me, but reluctantly.

"For being you, Bethany," she said to me, softly. "For always being there for me; for being the best friend I will *ever* have."

I could hear the emotion rippling her words, like still water suddenly disturbed by a flung rock. In any other time and place, I would have loved for this girl to have been my sister, or other close blood relation. It's truly seldom we find likeable, compatible people in life—I mean the *true* ones who are more familial than anything we know—and for me, Michelle was that person. It tears me up now, one week later, that that sentiment has been taken from us due to what I've become. Perhaps if Amy hadn't intervened, Michelle may have helped me overcome my ordeal.

"You're the bestest friend I've got, too," I said to her, and I knew she knew it. When my dad died, Michelle was my rock through that time.

"We'd better move—let's get to this party after the school disco," Michelle said as she slipped her arm through mine. "Come on, hold onto me in case these wings decide to take off!"

We walked together, happily, through the darkening street as little horrors ran door-to-door with bags of sweets, unaware of the teen zombie cheerleader and her companion—a sensual Angel of Death—that stormed by them in the most idyllic and determined of mortal moods.

SEVEN

THE school disco ran on a little later than what was planned. But it didn't matter because everyone appeared to be enjoying themselves right until they left. I did, especially; imagine if all your favourite horror film characters had an annual seminar— this would be it! There was Pennywise; several Freddy Kruegers; Michael Myers, and too many hockey masks to keep count, all running and dancing, and scaring one another. The music was loud; the gym-hall aether filled with dreaded, booming gongs and creaking doors, ghosts wailing and fingernails scraping. When Michael Jackson's *Thriller* blasted out of the speakers, many of the zombies in attendance tried to re-enact the famous dance scene in the centre of the hall, which led to hilarious results.

I really didn't have much time to dance or get involved in the games that were being played. I was more into behind-the-scenes work: prepping the prizes to giveaway, helping re-fill the snacks and drinks, and just generally trying to keep the place as tidy as possible. Doing all this work actually enabled me to see everything that was going on: who was dressed as what, where they were standing, and with whom.

Then, something happened. I can't tell if it was part of what Amy had called 'in the stars', but it certainly brought me to my attackers' attention. I know this now. And it wasn't Mr. Wiseman's fault, either.

I was arranging drinks on a table when the music cut off. The disco lights also came to a stop and a single light shone near the DJ's booth, where the principal was standing with a microphone, the light illuminating him. He had made the effort to dress up by wearing a hat with a fake, bloody axe through it. It was probably how he felt about his job sometimes. He asked for everybody's attention and the teen audience–at least, those who had been moving and grooving on the floor–simmered down for what he was about to say.

"Boys and girls!" he called out over the mic, his voice booming and crackling through the P.A. system. "I hope you're all having a great evening! We've seen lots of fantastic costumes; so many prizes given out for the best dancers. We really need to thank the pupil committee for putting on such a great event!"

As the clapping resonated around the hall, I had a sudden fear rise in me: a fear that the principal would call me out.

"And a big thank you to our birthday girl, Bethany Childs, who was responsible for seeing all of this come to life. A big hand for her also, please."

A second, not-as-loud round of applause sounded, and suddenly the light was shining on me. Everyone followed it and laid their eyes on me; I felt their stares burning, some interested, others not. In amongst those eyes, at least one pair had clocked onto me with deviant attention.

They now knew what I looked like.

I looked over at Michelle, which was hard to do with the light blinding me; she stood clapping–I could see her satin gloves smacking together. I tried to smile back at her, to show her I appreciated her support, but I was fast getting embarrassed and really wanted this moment to be over. Then, the light retreated and found its way back to the principal.

"Now, I need to go get some Aspirin," Mr. Wiseman said, "for I have a *splitting* headache!"

A round of booing sounded, like a verbal Mexican wave, as his audience was rattled by his bad joke. His lone laugh was then cut short as his mic died on him. He left the booth and returned to the side-lines.

Michelle came over to me.

"See?" she said, excitedly, "I told you this was your night!"

I poured each of us a drink of juice from a pitcher. It was blood orange flavour, likely chosen due to the name.

"You told him it was my birthday?"

Michelle flirted with my accusation. Her fluttering eyes gave it away.

"I might have said something…" she teased. "Anyway, they already know all that stuff–it's in the office files. I just felt *everyone* else had to know."

I play-growled at her, pretending I was angry that she had done so. But I knew Michelle–she had done it to be nice. If I wasn't so shy myself, I would have done the same.

Suddenly, the ominous opening to *Ghostbusters* began playing through the speakers, as everyone shouted its cult-psalm: "*Who you gonna call?*" before the eponymous cry of the song title blared.

"Come on!" Michelle shouted over the thumping score. "Let's get this one last dance in before it's time to leave. Our night's not over yet!"

I figured everything was running well enough for me to exert some energy on the dance floor. I allowed Michelle to pull me into the centre of the hall, where we rubbed shoulders with the profanest of phantoms, monsters, and devils, as circles of multi-coloured lights zipped over us from the laser machines. I managed to lose myself for those few minutes, as Michelle and I twirled one another under the combined musical chaos and lasers. Once, we bumped into each other, and I swear I heard her muttering something under her breath as our noses touched. I can't access matters of the heart, no matter how powerful my demonic power is. If there is any entity in Hell that's capable of such a feat, I'd say it would have to be Satan himself.

When we laughed right after we collided on the dancefloor, I thought I heard her say that she loved me.

EIGHT

IT was about half past nine when we began to wind things down at the disco. Pupils and staff alike had filtered out through the course of the evening, leaving behind mostly senior pupils and the principal, as well as some janitorial staff who kindly stayed behind to help clear up. The hall wasn't that bad. Nothing a good sweep and polish wouldn't clear up. There were enough refuse bags to help with the separating of the recyclable materials; the decorations were taken down and placed into boxes for next year.

By 10 P.M. we were more than halfway done. I thanked Michelle for helping also clear up. I could see she had lost some of that fresh look that she had when we first arrived; the hall had been too warm all evening, and not even opening the windows and emergency doors did much to cool us down. We were sweating like it was volleyball all over again. A quick trip to the girls' toilets meant we would be able to refresh ourselves.

"You coming, Bethany?" asked Michelle. "It's looking like it's nearly done."

I was throwing the last of the empty plastic juice cups into a bag. Mr. Wiseman, who was standing nearby with his axe-hat on, came over to us.

"Miss Childs, Miss Williams," he greeted both of us. "I can't begin to thank you for this evening. Everything went extremely well. There'll be merits awarded to both of you for your efforts—especially for staying to help clear up."

I placed the bag down, knackered. "Thank you, sir," I said.

"Now, why don't you two get home? Bethany, I'm glad that you chose to spend your birthday with us this evening. Others

45

wouldn't have been so kind and thoughtful."

"Well, I've kind of done this every year, sir," I began, even though he was right. I did have the option to forego the disco. "So, one more disco, before I leave here for good, wasn't really going to hurt."

"But, on your sixteenth as well?" he said, impressed, I think.

"Same date as last year's, sir!" I replied.

"You're an absolute credit to your par–" he stopped short, then, "–mother, Bethany Childs. To yours, also, Miss Williams, a credit."

It was obvious what he had been about to say, and even though it hurt, I wasn't affronted or upset or anything. The school faculty had known about my father's death–it was clearly just a slip of the tongue, following the way he praised me like that. I was more surprised that he remembered.

"Thanks, sir," Michelle responded, genuinely. Though she didn't get awarded as many merits as I did, whenever she was commended on something, she never looked at it lightly. And if she was being told that she was a credit to her parents, all the better for her. She had had enough to deal with in her young life–anything positive was a reward for her.

"Well, go on, you two, get safely home!" urged Mr. Wiseman, gently, playfully, pushing us out of the hall door into the corridor.

We giggled as he shoved; there was nothing in it, of course–he just wanted to be done with the mess and get home himself. Both hands placed in the smalls of our backs.

As we started off, he shouted something from behind us:

"Oh, girls: those outfits are spectacular! Miss Williams–Michelle–watch in those heels or you'll be nursing a broken ankle or two in the morning!"

Michelle waved back at him as we headed out the main school door. The cool air was inviting and we both stood for a few moments to breathe it in.

"It was like a furnace in there!" Michelle said.

I had to agree.

"I know–for a minute I thought we'd be doing the whole

'roasted marshmallows' thing, the way that heat was!"

"Ah-ah!" Michelle's exaggerated but playful reproach. "No real flames this year!"

I sucked in a soothing amount of air that chilled me right through.

"Well, shall we start walking?" Michelle suggested. "Lisa said it was Cameron's house for the party—no better time than now to get there!"

"We're not staying for long, are we?" I asked.

"As long or as short as you want, babe," Michelle said.

"Well, not too long. It *is* Halloween—who knows what dangers lie ahead?"

I stupidly presaged my own nightmare. At this point, Amy's 'release' had been provisionally granted from Hell (yes, believe me when I say it's a *very* orderly place). If and when my rape went ahead, she was entitled to walk upon Earth and take me under her wing under explicit retributory circumstances.

Whether I consented or not.

NINE

THE walk to the house party helped chill us a bit from the heat we suffered while we danced in the school hall. We had considered phoning a taxi, but we were so fuelled with excitement in our guises that we really just enjoyed the fun of the walk–of being the attraction. We must have looked a right pair, but it was funny to see people staring at us and laughing or complimenting us on our outfits. I'm sure one or two husbands and boyfriends gave us a second look as we passed them by.

The house wasn't that far from where we lived. We could hear the music and loud voices before we turned into the street.

We didn't know what to expect when we reached the gate: bodies lying drunk in the garden, windows fully opened or smashed, a TV set or drawer chest lying in the grass also. But it was nothing like that when we got there. Just the music, a thumping Eurodance mega mix, was a little on the loud side.

"Are you sure you want to go in?" I asked Michelle.

She let go of my arm so she could push open the garden gate.

"After you!" she said politely, as if I'd been royalty.

I moved first. I could feel my nerves shaking the fibre of my being as I strode, my pom-poms rustling against my legs. I then heard the rhythmic clicking of Michelle's heels as she followed me in.

"Should we knock or just go straight–"

Michelle's action answered my question. She walked by me and let herself in through the door, holding it open. It wasn't as if there were doormen taking numbers when we entered.

As one dance track ended, another was beginning to kick in. We had by then located the teenage son of the house owner, our classmate, Cameron—I even had a quick look for Lisa, so I could let her know that we had turned up.

It wasn't hard to tell that the parents in this house doted on their evidently only son, for the hallway was decorated with many photographs of him on the walls. Trophy winner for rugby, football and one or two others less physical let every visitor to the home know that their son had been at the sports game since he could walk and been very successful at it.

I lost track of Michelle as we weaved in and out of the path of student bodies. Some were kitted out in scary outfits, others less conservative. There was perhaps more skin on show than in Leatherface's Texas sitting room. It didn't matter to me who was wearing what, but I'd have bet anything that some mothers would have had reservations over the choice of their daughter's clothing had they seen what I saw. Certainly, the fathers would have.

Unbeknownst to me, as I was tailing Michelle, two black jump-suited skeletons were sniffing my tracks, one of whom had me marked earlier at the school disco.

"Hey, Michelle," I tried calling over the loud music and chatter. I could just make out the blonde top of her head and the two black wingtips of her costume accessory—it appeared she was heading to the kitchen.

I decided to catch her in there; instead of meandering through cigarette smoke, an air of deodorant, and stepping on empty beer cans, I just walked through the middle of the room. It was a spacious living room in an even more commodious house. If I had brought my cat along with me, I wouldn't have trouble swinging it in any of the rooms here.

I swiftly slipped by a fat Beetlejuice character and a normal-dressed reveller. I heard someone shout, "Show us your pom-poms!" but I didn't care to look back and acknowledge it. I was wondering if there was somewhere I could place my accessories so that I wasn't carrying them with me all night.

I entered the crowded kitchen and saw Michelle.

"Bethany!" she called. She was by the sink, drinking a glass of water.

I went to her.

"Sorry, I had to get some water."

"Don't worry about it," I said. "In fact, pour me one, too. I'm feeling a bit dry from that walk. It's hardly a July heat but it does drain you."

As Michelle poured a second glass from the tap, she asked, "Did you find that cow?"

"Who?"

"Lisa," she said.

"I've been looking for her, but I haven't seen her yet. She'll be around."

Michelle passed me the glass. The water was cold and refreshing. I sunk it quickly.

"Well, what now?" I asked.

"Come on," said Michelle, "let's go find somewhere less noisier."

"Less noisy!?" I corrected her.

"Okay, *Miss English*," she joked, "it's on you to find us somewhere *less noisy*, while I find us a couple of drinks, 'kay?"

"Do I have a choice in the matter?"

She slipped an arm around my waist, slid closer and in an unfamiliar voice whispered, "Not tonight." I say unfamiliar because when I looked up at her then, she had a vacant, dark look in her eyes as she leaned over me in her heels, almost as if she were being controlled by something else–some*one* else. Her voice unnerved me in that tone, low, like a growl, though not as menacing but just as unsettling.

I unravelled from her grasp and moved away, feeling a ripple of gooseflesh uninvitedly course through my body. I'm sure Michelle witnessed me shuddering, as if my own grave had been trampled on somewhere.

"I'll see you soon," she called after me.

I threw my hand up to signal to her that I'd heard and left that kitchen for the first and last time.

*****

If you'd met him, you would have agreed that he was the best dad ever, my father. *Of course, you'd say that!* you're thinking, but he really was. And there's not a day that goes by when I don't think of him in some way–in *any* way–to help keep his memory alive.

From the countless clichéd moments of him picking me up whenever I fell, or driving me to parties, or the three of us in warm summers driving to Aunt Jennifer's house, he was the definitive dad: funny, composed, tough on the inside and out, and loving. Never lifting his hands to either woman in his house, he just always seemed to know the right thing to say and do at the right time. And he rarely sugar-coated it by being patronising or condescending like some I've read or heard about. With him, you were as you are. He was my dad from that moment I was conceived, and not any time before it. That period of time belonged to him. From my moment of conception, that was when I became interested. Well, after I was born and grew up a bit first!

So, it was an immense, uncanny surprise to me when he appeared that night in the first of a deluge of chaotic dreams and nightmares, which I'll also talk about shortly. I always knew he'd remain at my side, even after his fatal heart attack, which removed him unkindly from the world, and ultimately, from our lives. I wasn't a believer in the supernatural–at least, not up until a week ago–but I suppose I've always had an open mind (as of late, as you know). Things that reminded me of him (his towering presence, his musky aftershave, an unlimited supply of bad 'dad' jokes) seemed to have never left the house; we felt him around us, watching us, protecting us. I think my mother and I needed to 'feel' him with us, to help cope with our grief.

It had crossed my mind afterwards that maybe Amy had some involvement in my father's 'appearance', but I found out that she hadn't, even though she had been aware of his passing. Perhaps she felt it a little too invasive and disrespectful to enter my life using my dead father's memory.

She did need me on her side, after all. A demon with a conscience!

In the first dream, he didn't say that much. A silhouette before a magnificent and calming light, he approached me in a manner that suggested he hadn't carried his deadly condition over to the other side. And before you ask, I am sure that it wasn't just a dream or a nightmare due to the trauma. The demonic power imbued in me lets me distinguish what is real and unreal in and outside of the world. His visits were genuine, and I know that he's waiting for my mother and me in Heaven–if I'm even allowed to enter.

So, in that initial dream, I found myself standing alone some distance from his darkened figure; despite my ordeal in the waking world mere hours before, I was surprisingly composed and accepting of this unnatural sight. I knew it was a dream and then, I didn't. In the dream, I knew something was wrong, and I knew it involved me. I was hurting physically; a feeling that was gradually seeping into the fabric of my night-time unconsciousness. I was squirming on my bed, tossing and turning, body temperature boiling and rising; my cat could sense that something wasn't right, and so she stayed at the door on all fours, tensed, and peeking in the gap.

I waited for the figure of my father to come to me, for I had noticed that he had started walking forward. There was no fear, no hesitation–I knew that in this situation, albeit unreal, I was safe.

"My Bethany," he called, as he became more visible the closer he got. The light from behind him pulsed; a sentient light created by a sentient, omnipotent being, no less.

"Dad?" I responded, heartily, hopefully.

"I know what has happened to you, and I am so sorry I could not prevent it. I wasn't permitted."

He turned and acknowledged the soundless light he now had an allegiance to, from a gesture he wanted me to notice and understand.

"Dad," my voice wavered, "what's going to happen to

me?"

Then, there was a chorus of whispering that seemed to rush from the light and straight to him, like a wind. My father turned his head slightly, but keeping his eyes fixed on me, and he was straining his hearing to pick up the onrushing murmurs.

"You need to stay strong, Bethany," he said; as if advising in some ghostly, fatherly way, or repeating just what he'd picked up from the whispers. "The darkness... the light... stay... strong."

The disembodied voices grew louder, or in number, and I saw my father's shape begin to recede. He was returning to that light, walking backward.

"But... d-d-dad," I heard myself stammering, afraid to lose him for a second time. "Don't go! I need you here! Daddy! *Dad!*"

The light continued to pulse and as my father walked back into the radiance, it surrounded him and took him.

Alone in the darkness of my dream, I stood, in tears.

Ever close, Amy waited impatiently for me.

TEN

CURIOSITY got the better of me sometime before midnight, while I was still clinging on to my birthday hours. I had lost Michelle again, despite meeting with her shortly after we separated in the kitchen to collect the drink she had found. I remember knocking it back; it was some colourful but foul-tasting liqueur, its name Russian or some other foreign brand. Michelle appeared to enjoy hers, but she was no drinker. She probably downed hers just to show off.

I had decided to venture upstairs to see if Michelle had gone up, a move I've since come to regret. The numbers had dwindled by then, and the music turned down, but was still loud and vibrating enough to be felt at the base of my eardrums. I climbed each step with heavy legs; foreboding isn't the word I'd use to describe the feeling that was all around and inside of me, but it's pretty damn close. I had no idea what awaited.

I stood on crisps and empty beer cans; was careful not to slip on the few beer bottles that lay atop the stairs. I chuckled as I thought of the movie *Home Alone*, imagining that the bottles were prepped and laid out for some unsuspecting, witless individual who'd have the misfortune of stepping and sliding on one, right down to the bottom of the stairs and breaking his coccyx.

"You guys give up, or you thirsty for more?!"

Foreboding…

The hallway went on for some length; several teenagers had remained, one or two up against the wall talking to another scouting for sex, cool and casual, hardly a sleepy-head in sight. I walked past them, head down and hurrying. I didn't wish to make contact with any of them for fear I'd have to speak to some drunk, mouthy teen looking to make fun of my Halloween costume.

Up ahead, I caught sight of a tall blonde wearing black slipping into a room. I thought about shouting out, thinking it was Michelle, but since I'd crept invisibly this far along the hallway, I didn't want to draw any attention to my presence now. I kept my head low and made for that room.

I pressed my palms against the door and gave it a good push, thinking it was one of the heavy, wooden doors that we had at ours. Instead, it gave way easily, almost as if it were pulled open from the inside at the same time. I half stumbled before bumbling completely into what was an adults' bedroom. There was no light on inside the room. And strangely, there was no tall blonde present either, just an herbal, smoky haze…

…and, four skeletons sitting on a futon across from me, with glow-in-the-dark bones on their jumpsuits. They made no noise, no laughter or concern as I had burst in; they could have been ghastly *kuroko* and this their kabuki stage.

They were smoking, and from the smell of it, it didn't smell like anything legal. The pungent waft of cannabis was the haze in the room.

"You lost, sweets?" one of the skeletons enquired, before all four of them then burst into laughter. Unfunny, moronic snorting.

They finished passing the joint around, and as I made to turn back the way I came, one of them shot up off the futon and quickly closed the door.

"Born in a barn, babe?" this skeleton said as he eased the door shut with his full weight against it. His resulting glare pinned me to the spot.

"I'm just looking for my friend," I said in a low but determined voice. "I thought I saw her walk in here."

"No one else in here but us, sweets," said the skeleton who had first spoken. "And you."

I was nervous and worried in equal measures. I was *certain* I saw Michelle come in here.

"I saw a blonde girl come in here," I said, aware of the skeleton who kept guard by the door. "Her name's Michelle."

"I don't think we know her, sweets," said the first skeleton again, "and if she'd been a blonde, I think we'd have remembered seeing her. Right, lads?"

They all answered him with a lackey-like response. I felt sick being caught up in their presence. I mean, why was this one *still* in front of the door? He had no business being there. Then, he spoke:

"Stay here with us, chill for a bit. It's getting a bit shit out there anyway. All the good stuff's gone home."

"Not all of it," one of the other seated skeletons piped up.

"No, I'm fine, I'd better go and find my friend, she'll be missing me, and she will come looking." I had blurted this out as a kind of warning to them, but it was soon clear that they weren't heeding it. It was evident when Skeleton Doorman reached across and grabbed a magazine from a nearby dresser and folded it in half to stub under the door as a doorstop. To enhance its newfound, makeshift purpose, he kicked it under, further prohibiting the door from opening.

"A draft excluder!" he announced after the third and final kick which tore some of the pages.

The other three laughed at this inane remark, but I was now petrified. I thought, *Maybe I should smile or laugh with them, and they'll remove it and let me go 'cause they'll see I have a sense of humour, too.* But there was no chance that was going to happen. They were locking me in with intention.

"Can you open the door?" I tried to be reasonable and polite. At this stage, I didn't wish to do anything to exacerbate the situation or provoke them.

"Can't," replied Skeleton Doorman. "It'll let the heat out."

"It's hotter than hell in here!" said one of the other futon skeletons (to be more general, Hell is mostly ice and darkness). Skeleton One had gone all quiet. In fact, if it wasn't for the glow-in-the-dark bones on his jumpsuit, I'd have thought he'd gone out of the room completely.

"Look," I began, stupidly appealing to their buggered senses of reasoning, "you'd better let me out of here, okay? My friend will be out there looking for me."

"Well, then," spoke Skeleton One, finally. "If she knocks asking, we'll let her in."

He stood up when he finished speaking, joined by the other two who were seated beside him, and spoke again, trying to sound funny.

"Until then, why don't you stay and play with us?"

"I can't… I don't have time to play silly fucking games!" I raised my voice at them, more out of fear and alarm than anger. "Just stay the fuck away from me or I'll scream for help."

One of the futon skeletons, as if on cue, went and checked that the windows were shut. The light from the lamp-post outside was the only light that came in through the windowpane, an artificial orange glow that trailed along the carpet and onto the bed's valance.

"Ain't double-glazing a bitch!" said the skeleton near the window in a terrible, mock American accent. He tapped on the glass with a bony knuckle. "Nothing gets in… nothing gets out."

I tried running for the door, a futile attempt. But Skelton Doorman remained at his post while the other remaining futon skeleton tackled me from the side, swerving so we crashed against the big double bed behind us. I banged my side against the corner of the divan base, which sent a jolt of pain through my torso. I tried to scream but a sweaty hand covered my mouth. I attempted to bite it but no luck. As one fiend pressed his weight upon me to stop me from pushing forward, another grabbed me from behind under my arms and pulled me up onto the bed. I thrashed, kicked, kneed, whatever my legs could do to defend myself against the gang attack, but with four-against-one it was useless.

I could hear them, getting excited, whispering things like, *"Look at what she's wearing!"* and *"It'll be easy enough to rip off!"* As I felt their hands forcibly grab hold of my clothing, my zombie costume, and tear it to bits from my gooseflesh-riddled body, I fought between continually striking out and trying to scream for help, or just lay there until they were done.

I had started with the former, then begrudgingly settled with the latter.

With one attacker forcibly holding my arms above my head so I couldn't throw my fists or swipe my nails to gouge out their eyes and my exposed breasts are being grabbed and fondled and nipped at by teeth and lips, and I can feel the strong muscles in my legs aching and weakening, straining to fight against them being prised apart by even stronger, eager hands…

All this time…

All this time, Amy knew and was watching.

After one, two, three and the fourth individual penetrations weakened my body and its fight, I lay motionless on the ruffled bed covers once they were done. I hadn't screamed for help. I hadn't fought with everything I had. But God knows I tried.

Finished with me, they eventually kicked out the magazine doorstop and one by one, the skeletons left me on that bed to rot. I lay with my head to the side, watching through tears as the rain began rapping against the window. My mouth ran dry. The cannabis smoke made me giddy.

The demon was now permitted to walk the Earth. It had work to do.

Hallowed be thy name.

Salvation in mine.

ELEVEN

IT'S *all in your head*, my inner voice was saying to me, trying to make me make sense of what just happened. Although the gang attack in total took no more than thirty minutes or so, I felt like I had been lying there for an eternity. My wrists were still throbbing from their restraints, my underarms stretched and searing with electrifying pain from being pulled taut, as if I'd been subjected to my own memory foam-bottomed torture rack. I can't begin to describe the pain that was viciously dealt to my groin area, but I think you get the idea. Between my thighs it was sticky and wet with blood and semen.

My breathing came in hard, rasping, breaths, and I could feel my heart thudding against my chest as if it were trying to tear free itself from its bloody chamber. I wanted to sit up, alone in the darkness with the rain the only sound I could hear, but fear, anger, and humiliation kept me bedbound for some time.

Eventually I managed to roll over onto my side, trailing the covers with me, cocooning myself within the cold duvet sheet. My dress was utterly ruined. I rubbed my feet together–they had removed my shoes and socks; I could feel my skin, despite it being numb, and it was cold. If any passers-by were to pop their head in and I looked as still and expired as a dead body, then this room was my morgue. A setting that couldn't have been paired any truer with the way I was feeling: that my life as I knew it, had ended.

*****

It was almost 1 A.M. when I left that bedroom, the clock in

the hall let me know. I had picked up my clothing, carried them over my bruised, trembling forearms, and had managed to slip into my shoes. The laces were snapped so they were loose on my feet. I wearily–painfully–shuffled along the corridor, where not a single soul stood. With every small step I took it felt like I had weights strapped to my thighs and calves. My jacket, thrown over in an attempt to conceal the naked skin that was exposed through my ripped costume. I trudged along without a care for anything or anyone but myself.

There were voices from downstairs that carried up to me as I waited to descend the stairway. I didn't wish to come across anyone in my current state; but then, I also needed to get help. Where was Michelle? Was she still here? Had the four skeletons bragged about their crime before leaving? Had anybody known I was in that room?

The voices were not important-sounding, just jibber-jabber from drunken teenage mouths. I figured it to be the dregs of the party, desperately clinging on to the event's activities before having to go.

I had figured out how I'd leave. I would go down the stairs as far as I could, then when I saw a chance, I'd speed-walk past everyone and head for the front door, no eyeballing, no verbals.

And, that's what I did, Sans impediment.

I must have looked a right sight as I scooted past the cosy gathering of bodies huddled on the couch. They all stared at me as I rushed past, head down without seeking or making eye contact with any of them. As I grabbed the front door handle and pulled it open before escaping into the wet, soundless, cold layer of night, I heard someone ask, "Who the fuck was that?"

The reply: "Looked like a crazy-assed cheerleader. From Hell."

They had no idea.

TWELVE

SO, it was clear that Michelle was no longer at the party. I didn't care. I just wanted to be home, away from this horror. I thought about going to the police but that somehow seemed just as terrifying. Besides, I was freezing, and I felt really unclean. But, should I bathe with the evidence of the rape that was still dripping down my legs? It would wash it away, surely, and no one would believe me. I had the bruises visible all over, but they could have come from anywhere.

I picked up my pace as I marched along the darkened streets, afraid yet staying vigilant of any other horrors that might have been lurking. My hair was soaked and the shreds of costume that remained felt as if they were just strips of bunting slung over my body. My bare legs wobbled with each thumping step, as the muscles up and down them refused to work properly; despite the cold, the muscle groups in those limbs, drilled beyond exertion, were throbbing and wasted–I could only hope they would carry me home.

I had considered heading to Michelle's first, as I would pass her house on the way to mine. Her bedroom was on the bottom floor; I would need to give the window a light tap to see if she was inside. But the pain searing through each of my legs and groin didn't warrant this off-shoot excursion, so I continued home.

I eventually made it, hassle-free. The rain was battering down heavily now, and if my face wasn't so numb from the pain I felt inside, it surely would have been stinging due to the ice-cold raindrops that the sky saw fit to pour over me. I managed to grip the door handle and use it as support to hold me up whilst I found the house key in my jacket pocket. I slid it into the lock and twisted it to unlock the door.

The hallway, as I expected, was in complete darkness. I stood at the threshold for a minute or two, I think, blankly staring into this darkness, as if awaiting permission to enter. I was so tired and exhausted that I thought there were things in that blackness ahead of me that were swirling and forming shapes that had no earthly matter. My eyes were beat, and I was drained almost to the point of collapsing; I had to find excess strength to move and get up to my room: my place of sanctuary.

I stepped in, closing the door quietly behind. The darkness immediately hid everything as my eyes fought to adjust to it. Still, there were things that couldn't stop swirling in there. I moved to the staircase, catching a glimpse of something that briefly glimmered in the kitchen. The decorations from my birthday—they had been left up. That got me thinking, was my mum home? Did she have to work overnight? I knew that her job meant she had to attend various meetings, but she hadn't mentioned anything to me about going away, especially on my birthday. And the door was locked—but then, she'd have thought I was sleeping over at Michelle's, which was what I should have been doing.

I climbed the stairs and reached out to the wall for the light switch. I hesitated before switching it on. It's funny, because I was starting to grow so fond of the dark, that it seemed almost like I was turning my back on it when I pressed on the light. Instantly, the light blasted away those swirling shapes. It hurt my eyes so that I lifted one of my weakened, bruised arms to shield them from the brightness.

It was as if I was beginning to despise the light.

My mother's bedroom door was closed, and I didn't fancy opening it and exposing her to how I was, not now, even though my heart was weakened and cried out for comfort and safety. I just wanted to be in my bed, alone, and forget about what happened.

My door was closed, too. I always left it open for the cat to come and go. My mum knew that, too, so I didn't think she had closed it intentionally, if she had at all. I reached down and pulled the handle, and my cat instantly bolted out of the gap. My bed covers were messed up and my window was open, letting in a fair amount of cold wind to air and refresh my room.

I threw down the rags I was carrying and sat on my bed, forlorn and desolate. I wanted to scream, cry, tear my hair out, but the most calming thing I thought of doing was removing my clothes. Miraculously, throughout my ordeal, my half-heart pendant had remained around my neck. I unclipped it, dropping one end whilst pulling on the other. The thin chain fell down the space between my breasts, until I dropped it into my hand, holding it tightly, before shoving it under my pillow for safekeeping. I peeled the costume from my body in the strips that remained, the torn red and black dress, and without thinking, threw it upon my father's wicker chair. I kicked off my loose shoes; they struck the wall but made a quiet double *thump!* I was still freezing so I didn't fancy sitting any longer in this ice-cold room; I got up and headed for the bathroom, against my better judgement, for a hot shower.

THIRTEEN

I have already gone over the dream of my father's visitation. But now that Amy is in the picture, I better start moving toward the horrific revenge she made me–sorry, *empowered* me to–carry out. But do not ask me to prove anything to you or reveal any of the power I wield. My story should be enough and the events I relay to you honest-to-God did happen. Why, there are five dead or maimed individuals to verify that! Not that I'm proud of the way we handled things–remember at the beginning of this story, when I told you that revenge is sweet but also how it's dangerous? It's wild and if you try to stick a leash on it, it will just break free and… well, you get the idea. I'm in no position to belittle or insult your intelligence.

I awoke the next morning with the mother of all headaches. Plus my vagina, brutalised to my attackers' content one sleep ago, throbbed and itched. I really needed to consider getting medical attention in case there were any nasty deposits left behind.

The time on my clock read 8:11 A.M. I had no desire to get up and dressed for school. Similarly, that sentiment stretched to every other aspect of my life. I wanted to just lay there in bed, forever.

My door pushed open slightly; I didn't know who or what to expect to see. The attractive brunette, Amy, or my mum. The answer was revealed as my view dropped to the floor: Tabby. The feline was creeping in, watching me with whatever curiosity cats possess of their human owners. Only, this morning she appeared to be warier. She took too many steps reaching my bed, stopping every couple to keep an eye on me, as if I were about to do something untoward. Could she sense the way I was feeling? Had she been present when this woman found her way into my room, likely through some mystical portal? Or was it just me being paranoid and anxious, looking the worse for wear, and the cat's instincts were sensing it?

She leapt up onto the bed, on top of the covers where underneath my feet lay.

"Good morning, you," I croaked, my mouth and lips dry.

The feline seemed neither fussed nor fretted. She viewed me again with those jade marbles before curling up and laying down.

"What did you see last night, eh?" I asked the cat. "Who was that woman? Was she real?"

The cat lifted its head and pricked its ears, indicating as if it knew what I was saying. Of course, I wasn't expecting it to talk back to me, but something weird had happened in my room during the early hours and I'm certain my cat knew of it.

I reached down and gave one of her front paws a gentle squeeze, just to show her I was okay.

There was no sunlight starting to shine through the window, no birds tweeting overhead outside; in fact, it was cold and breezy, and most likely still wet, if it had continued to pour overnight.

It was November 1st.

FOURTEEN

MY mum got up and out of her bedroom just before 9 A.M., and as much as I hoped she would stick her head in the door to see if I was here, she never did. I wanted to scream out, shout her in, but something in my mind told me not to. I didn't know if it was the fear and anger of telling her about what had happened to me and having to remember, or if she would want to call the police and get me to the hospital. I think I was plain scared to face anyone. I feel somewhat comfortable telling you my story because at least we're not face to face, eye to eye, but to sit and be asked all the questions of the night before—I mean, I've seen the movies, read the stories. And the conviction rate for such an appalling crime? It was less than desired.

So, I stayed in bed, as quiet as a mouse. I heard my mum going about her business downstairs, getting ready to leave for work, before I heard the crunching together of keys as she grabbed them from the hook on the wall. She left around half-past ten; I dashed to the toilet, unable to hold my pee in any longer. It stung when I urinated. After wiping clean, I was horrified to see there was blood streaked on the tissue. Flushing that away, I returned to my bedroom and hid back under the duvet.

Shortly after, I heard the front door opening. I heard:

"Bethany! Bethany, you home?"

It was Michelle.

Thank God. A friend, someone I could trust. Someone who could help me. But, did I have the strength to tell her the truth? To open to her the way she did me. I knew she would believe me. But she would also advocate the involvement of

66

the police and right now, unlike some, I just didn't feel I had that in me.

She began walking upstairs. I sat up in bed, trying to look as normal as possible.

When she reached the landing, I heard her in her boots, thumping along the floor to my room. Her pretty blonde head popped into view in the doorway.

"What's happening, sleepy-head?" she boomed, all smiles.

I put on the biggest, fakest smile I thought I could fool her with.

"Nothing much. Slept in, didn't I? Bit of a sore stomach as well, actually. Was up for a bit during the night, sick."

She came into the room fully, shooing my cat along the bed so she could sit down.

"I didn't see you this morning, and since you're the only teenage girl in the world without a mobile phone–dunno how or why!–I couldn't reach you and *I* was already late–"

"Okay, okay!" I pleaded, playfully, "I get it! Maybe I'll get one off the birthday money my mum's giving me."

She looked around the room. Then, I remembered: my costume! Amy had it in her possession whilst she spoke with me, and now it was gone. Did she still have it? Had it fallen from the chair? I looked over at the chair and the floor beneath it but couldn't see anything.

"So, what's wrong with you, really?"

I breathed out, hard and heavy, totally emptying my lungs.

"I just… I can't…Michelle, I need *help*…"

I was never any good at hiding my emotions. In one massive, tear-filled, outpour, I spilled everything: thinking I saw her going into the room at the party, the door being stubbed shut, being held against my will, and the four skeleton-suited monsters who hurt me. One at a time.

At this point, I was unsure whether the encounter with Amy had been real or not, so I chose to omit her appearance from my terrifying, expressive deluge.

*****

Michelle sat with me for the whole of my story; and why wouldn't she have? We cried together last year over her agonising story, and we cried together now over mine.

"Have you been to the police?" she asked, half-enquiring, the other half demanding.

"No, not yet," I said, "but I'm not sure I want to."

Michelle almost jumped from the bed. "But, Bethany, you *have* to! We can't let those fucking bastards get away with this!"

"They won't," I tried to reassure her, "but I need to do it in my own time."

She looked at the cat then back at me. "I'm so sorry, Bethany, if I hadn't said to go to that party…"

"It's not your fault, Michelle. I was in the wrong place at the wrong time."

"But that doesn't make it right for them to do that to you!"

During the outpour, Michelle had run to the toilet to fetch some tissue; I had wept my way through most of it but was still using some to dry my eyes.

"I know, and I promise I *will* get help," I said.

"You have no idea who they are?"

"I think maybe one or two go to our school, but the others were older, maybe late teens."

"I don't want to interfere, Bethany–I know you didn't push me, but this is worse–but you need to make sure you don't forget all the facts. The police will need them to catch these… monsters."

Monsters. If only Michelle knew what a true monster was. Sure, some men and women of the world balanced on the periphery of the notion–the Dahmers, Hindleys, and Bathorys, to name such a few–each conducting their own unspeakable, heinous crimes, but if you only could take a stroll through the scorched ruins of Hell (as I have), you will see the shadows of ancient, once-powerful angels grovelling at the feet of their new dark masters, and you'll pray that they won't see *you.*

"Don't worry, there's no way I'm going to forget."

"I still think you should call the police. Now. Even go to the hospital. You don't know if they-"

"Gave me anything–yeah, I had thought of that. Please trust me, I'll fix this. I don't know how, yet, but I will."

Michelle enveloped my cold hands with hers.

"I do trust you. I always have–it's why we've made it this far as friends. What about your mum? You need to tell her."

"I'll do that, too. Just let me–" I sighed, long and hard "– deal with this in my own time."

"You've suffered a major trauma, Bethany! It's not like you've scraped your knee or broken your arm–you were *raped!*"

"I know what it was," I said, thus ending that line of conversation.

She leaned toward me and kissed my cheek. In that instant, I remembered when Amy was standing over me just hours before, sweeping aside my hair. Oh, how the touch from each woman had set my heart racing! It was likely from knowing I had the love and support from Michelle, and whatever this Amy was planning on doing that appeared to be for my benefit, that I began developing feelings for either.

We let the rest of the morning and afternoon skip by uneventfully, taking turns petting the cat and consoling one another. But we each had die-hard nagging questions pertaining to my assault, and I, over when I'd be seeing Amy again.

FIFTEEN

ALTHOUGH it's discouraged, I decided to keep the assault quiet. I didn't want anyone knowing about it, but on the other hand I was fucking livid that it happened. I cried most of that Tuesday when Michelle sat with me, right through into the late evening. When my mother came home, she found me in that distressed state in my bed; I managed to pass it off as severe period pain. She kindly fetched me some painkillers and kept me hydrated with plenty of glasses of water every half hour or so.

My cat, Tabby, kept a vigil on my bed. I remember her laying curled all snug, sinking into that space between my feet. Those jade marbles were halfway to sleep, until it hit 9 P.M. when they suddenly sprung open, alert, and instinctive to whatever invisible presence was disturbing it.

"What's wrong, Tabby? Is she here again?"

Then, upon my father's wicker chair, a feminine shape began to materialise, like a disengaging cloaking device, a presence that was forming the outline of a clothed body. It was surreal: smooth long legs came to life before my eyes, half covered by that angelic-type tunic she had worn the night before; and this time, a decoration of sorts, an item of imperial jewellery tied to her robe around her waist, but which would be more fitting to wear upon your head, something that I'd not spotted before: a crown that sparkled as each section solidified.

When she finished uncloaking out of the air, I remained still, with my head on the pillow, taking in the sight with unbelievably calm composure. Michelle was right when she told me I had been through a major trauma. And I certainly wasn't out of the woods yet. Perhaps this was the effects of shock that sexual assault victims experience, that the brutality of the attack was somehow manifesting itself in the guise of this fair woman; a woman whose beauty I admired, but who may have been the physical embodiment of my anger and fear.

"Hello, Bethany," Amy said, warmly.

Well, if she had been an apparition, or emotional thought projection—an embodiment of my feelings—she certainly remained a verbal one.

"How did you do that?" I managed to speak some sense.

"A little magic where I come from—" she replied, excitedly, as if it were a big secret and one I wasn't allowed in on "—but I'll skip the pleasantries, Bethany—we've got a revenge to work out!"

I had been straddling the border between being asleep and awake, but with this shock announcement I felt myself being thrown back into the here and now (well, back then and there) of things.

"*Amy*," I uttered, without much belief, for I had no idea if that was her real name, "what do you want from me? Why are you here?"

"Two things, child: I know what happened to you last night in that room. I *felt* your fear, your hurt, your isolation, and your anger, the latter of which leads me here. For you."

She spoke confidently, with honed mannerisms in her hands and eyes. She sounded as if reciting a speech designed to rally the numbers.

"My *what?*" I queried. "Did Michelle tell you what happened at the party?"

"Nobody told me," Amy replied. "It was always going to happen. It was just a matter of time."

I sat up, eager to hear more. Despite knowing absolutely nothing about this woman, and having just witnessed the unthinkable, the unbelievable, I felt I would allow my mind to exact whatever stress relief it insisted to see me through.

"You know about what they did to me?"

Amy, ever the comforting psychic, placed a hand on mine.

Again, smooth and delicate.

"I know what they did. I *saw* it, child."

I turned away from this… ghost, afraid that she would see me cry.

"I… I don't know what to do," I mumbled, sobbing.

"Bethany Childs, take my hand," she ordered, but patiently, allowing me time. "For *I* know what to do."

*****

As the night wore on, Amy stayed at my side, enthralling me with a glimpse into who she really was. She spoke to me about things I had no idea I would ever get to know—that *anyone* would ever get to know—for she spoke of original religion and of her place in it. She was quite the traveller, it seemed.

Although she never openly admitted she was a demonic entity, there were clues dotted about in her tales and of company she kept—certain royal names that I now know to be standout text in literature such as *The Lesser Key of Solomon*. I have no doubts, now, that she was once engaged in battles and predicaments—sexual or otherwise—with the sovereign rulers of Hell and Earth and Heaven, tangling with both the elite and the mediocre in each realm. But I feel like I'm repeating myself; I have already told you what she was like, and this is for certain: she could talk the talk and had walked the walk.

She dismissed the stories of satanic rituals and abuse on Earth, saying only the undeserving and heedless resorted to gruesome acts; Satan demands purity and conviction, among other inanities, in his servants. Ultimately, he did not want the disturbed and retarded flying his flag on Earth.

I did feel awkward taking in her supernatural archives; if it had been my mind struggling to deal with its current state then I would have had no idea where all this nonsense came from. As fate had it, it was all real, and I know now that the majority of what she said is true. Amy winced if I mentioned Jesus, and she demanded that I never say his name again.

She talked for many hours more, before she decided that my transformation should begin.

"So, I'm here because we need to do something to those vermin that hurt you."

Intrigued, I said, "I can go to the police."

"But you won't, and what use is it now? You've washed away the evidence, and for all the good your law enforcement will do, there's no guarantee that there'll be justice."

"And you're going to help me?"

"Of course. Deep down, I know you want me to. I know *I* want to. I've waited years to deliver the punishment deserving of these foul creatures' behaviour, Bethany."

"What do you plan to do? Have us convince them to confess?"

"Nothing of the sort, child! Why, your saviour–" she spat out imaginary phlegm, disgusted at the fact she had to refer to Jesus "–opined turning the other cheek in terms of being an assault victim! Do you think it would be exemplary of you to return to them? That they would see it as something other than rewarding?"

I shook my head.

"Then, hear what I have to say. There's going to be a big change, child. If you agree to it, I will bestow upon you unlimited power from my own infernal cabal; together, we will take back what they stole from you, and see that they *never* do it to anybody else."

"I don't get it–what *infernal cabal?*"

"Child, say that you'll agree to my intercession!"

"But what if–"

"We don't have much time, Bethany Childs! Accept my offer, have your revenge; make them suffer for what they did to you!"

"I don't–"

She smiled, flirtatiously, lowering her voice to a velvety whisper, as if she were coaxing me into that infernal cabal.

"You don't have to do anything but say yes."

And with that, she climbed into bed with me.

SIXTEEN

NO, she didn't fuck me per se, but she might as well have. At first, her hands wandered over my body; I could feel a strange, electrifying sensation course through me at her touch, a dizzying awareness that felt almost as if I was being healed. It's strange to describe, but to liken it to something that you may be familiar with: codeine, or an illegal high. A warm wave of relaxation just washing over you once you'd popped a pill or two. *For the pain.* But that was it—there was no pain throbbing anymore, it had been pressured away or teased out by Amy's wonderful massage technique. She lay close to me, flat, sliding over so that our noses touched, and our eyes met. I had no desire to push her away. Her hand found its way over my knees, her fingers sliding up my thigh before she was palm-against my vagina. She didn't remove my underwear as she rubbed but used her fingers instead to pull the thin fabric to the side and slide her fingers in.

There was still no pain. In fact, the insertion caused me to raise my knees in pleasure as she worked her finger in and out; then two, maybe three. She kissed me on the lips, and I felt something in me *change*; the pain, the anger, the fear and hurt, all decimated as we lay side-by-side in our heated embrace.

"Do you accept it?" Amy whispered, her fingers in and out, our bodies undulating under the heated cover, rippling with unnatural–*super*natural–delight.

"I… do," I managed to exhale, her infernal power rushing through me.

"Then, you are mine!"

She thrust harder and I bucked a little; I had been concerned that someone would walk in as we were doing our thing, but the constant tiny surges of pleasure that Amy fingered into me kept me from worrying more.

Suddenly, her eyes burned intensely red, like two golf-ball-sized orbs that were lighting up the interior of our duvet bivouac. There was heat emanating from them that warmed my face. She pulled her fingers out of me and I looked down… and suddenly I wasn't looking at my legs, but where my feet should have been there was a cavernous black hole that somehow, I was standing over. I may very well have been hovering over it, even though I could still feel as if I were laying down.

"Amy…" I whimpered, grabbing hold of her, afraid I'd fall into that blackness.

"This is where your power lies!" she said, like a gameshow host teasing me with prizes. "I want you to have it! And I *will* give it to you!"

She put the fingers that had been in me into her mouth, sucking them; I heard a raucous commotion rising from the dark pit underneath us. It could have been an excitable outburst from whatever entity occupied the nethermost reaches of its dwelling. I continued to look down, completely afraid and disbelieving, despite all that I'd seen.

It was then I noted that Amy had been holding my hand this whole time, keeping me afloat. I looked at those flame-red spheres that were her eyes, and I knew just what she had been doing.

"Don't be afraid, Bethany, *this* is who you really are!"

Then she let go of my hand.

I plummeted straight to Hell.

Never take your own revenge, beloved, but leave room for the wrath of God, for it is written, "Vengeance is mine, I will repay," says the Lord.

B~~eth~~any Chiller

Romans 12:19

A VIRGIN OF VENGEANCE
2nd NOVEMBER

ONE

SO, now that you've been given the bones of my horrendous story, how does it feel? Traumatic, isn't it? But there's still a lot to be said and a lot that was done, for you to understand the truth. It's now up to me to start 'meating' the skeleton of this tale.

I'm still in this quarry behind my home; there's a light on in my mum's room that I can see, and in the darkness around me small animals and *other* shapeless things are moving around. There is still no sign of Amy. My eyes continue to burn to provide light and warmth. It's no fun writing all this down–for either of us–but it's helping me to continue coping with the surreal change.

But I don't know what to do anymore. Will this power diminish, or–as I mentioned earlier–will I be alive to see the end of the world with it? And I'm not talking about a nuclear war or anything like that; I mean, when we've exhausted and pilfered all of Earth's resources; when our air and water become contaminated by deadly pollution and the ozone layer weakens entirely, I very well may be *the* last person on Earth, surveying the devastation we knew for decades was coming. Maybe then Amy will return for me.

Although, it is not the future I saw for myself.

Amy had just finished pleasuring me in my room, before dropping me–literally–into Hell. Largely not the apocalyptic Hell from centuries-old paintings or past scholars' descriptions, but the Revelations version (I assumed); it was cold there. There was a terrible, acrid odour, like a million matchheads had been struck here moments before; sulphur became the air around me as I knelt on the ground in the eerie

79

darkness, sobbing, for whatever was shifting about me in the shadows I pleaded to leave me alone. And despite not seeing much at all, I had this desolate feeling rising; despair, dread– that this little spot in which I was sited was merely a sample of what the 'wider' ground felt like. There was little (un)natural light that came from somewhere, enabling me to see at least a few centimetres around me. But, the darkness here–indeed, it was the original pit in which the Archangel Michael helped fill with Heaven's many original oppressors–akin to God's shadow. In the growing gloom in which I sheltered, it was clear that God had turned His back on me here, and I wondered if this was what it was like to be Satan: sitting in *that* shadow, lost and angry, and hurting.

A booming voice called out, like a judge attempting to pacify his courtroom.

"Bethany Childs, you have been sequestered from humanity to serve Hell's purpose."

I lifted my head, but sight here was useless. It was near impossible to see who or what was addressing me from somewhere in the dark.

"Why?" I managed to blurt out.

Shuffling sounds, like a great big beast moving around, craving a better position.

"You are damned, but you have been chosen. In our servant's custody you will operate under an alias–this, *you* have agreed."

I shook my head.

"That's not why I'm here," I started to argue back.

"But it is. And thus, *here you are.*"

A hot rush of wind wafted over my face that could have been exhaled breath from an unseen, gaping mouth. The shapes shifting in the dark seemed closer and eager than before.

"Where is that woman; Amy?" I asked, trying my best to exude confidence to the disembodied voice as a form of protection; feeble, though, it seemed.

"Waiting for you," it replied, and the words reverberated

through my entire body, ringing true and loud and clear.

Another lashing of odourless hot air; hotter than the last, indicating that whatever was exhaling it was getting closer, for the more intense I felt it, the nearer its source was becoming.

The ground started to shake; indeed, I wasn't entirely sure what I was kneeling upon—I presumed I had landed on something broad and touchable, based on the hardness of the ground underneath me. But what, I couldn't determine; I could have been perched upon a totem pole with a thousand-foot drop around me had I the courage to stand up and take a few steps. As it happened, I kept still.

I was tired. Tired of feeling miserable and aimless—if these entities were real and not just some hallucinatory episode concocted by my mind breaking down and going to shit, then I would acquiesce without resistance.

Flames shot up in a circle pattern around me, making me look as if I were the conjured subject of a demonic ritual. The bright upright fires—nine in total—caged me in.

Despite this enflamed circular cell, I felt no scorching heat or discomfort of any kind. Then I noticed, standing on the outside of the flames, Amy, looking as she had in my room, tall, beautiful, with flowing hair and glowing, glowering ruby-red eyes. Nearby, another entity was hovering about a meter from the ground, hooded yet watching in my direction. Both creatures were facing me before Amy stepped, untouched, through the flames and stood with me in the centre. I stood up at last, and face-to-face we touched.

"Bethany Childs!" she called above the hissing and roaring of the heatless flames. "You are now in my infernal cabal!"

I lost power in my legs and fainted into Amy's waiting arms. But before I completely blacked out, I heard her blessing me with that bastardisation of my angelic name:

"I christen and condemn you: *Bethany Chiller!* They *will* know your name!"

TWO

I awoke the next morning feeling completely mentally refreshed. Reborn, almost. A nerve-tingling sensation surged through me, a bit like anxiety and frustration, that not enough was getting done to avenge my horrific rape.

The one mistake that Amy had made was thinking I was going to wholly indulge in the creature I was to become. I may have pampered myself by now with Hell's merchandise, subscribing to its satanic membership with an impunity never seen before, but back then I was fearfully reluctant of embracing this newfound being, *Bethany Chiller*. It was me, and it wasn't.

I got out of bed at 9 A.M. I was alone in the house again, so I took my time showering. Still, that anxious, frustrated feeling was playing havoc with my nerves; I wanted to smash everything I looked at: ornaments, doors, mirrors. I was losing control of myself, something that Amy had foresaw and was betting highly on.

I returned to my room and closed the door. I caught sight of my reflection in the mirror. I looked the same as ever on the outside. As I stared, and the seconds moved, I grew more annoyed. Everything suddenly flooded back: my father's death and dream visit; the party rape; Amy's initiation—my hands fisted as I felt that unknown power surging through my veins. I screamed out loud, venting my anger, and punched the mirror; the glass shattered into hundreds, thousands, of little shards, raining down over my feet.

It didn't hurt.

And it left no marks on my fist. No blood, no cuts, no scrapes, despite the mess it created. I stood there, towel-wrapped and breathing heavily, like a model in a bathroom sales brochure, only angrier, grimmer, looking at the fragmented reflection. Some glass had remained in the frame, like rotted teeth in a rotten mouth.

I stared at the glass shards below, wishing I'd never broken the mirror. It was a decent mirror–had been. My arms hanging by my sides, dejected, I turned away from the mess and sat on my stool. I had no desire to break the mirror on my drawer set.

Then, something occurred to me. A little voice, a suggestion floating around in my brain, hunting for attention, saying I could *fix* the mirror. Not by buying a new one or by gluing the pieces back together, but just by *thinking* I could. I swivelled on the stool and fixed my gaze on the glass shards on the carpet. Intently I stared, and the larger pieces began to shake, shimmering in the natural light that came in from the window. I began to get excited, since there was no other movement in the house that could be making the glass move like that.

A few moments longer and those larger fragments were lifted by my thoughts. They were picked up and suspended in the air as if held by invisible hands. The grainier stuff remained on the carpet, rendered useless by my fist. But, that too, started piling together, minute shards that could cause hell if inhaled.

As I concentrated, thinking nothing other than putting the mirror back to its original state, the hanging glass one at a time returned to its place within the frame on the back of the door, like a crooked jigsaw, built by the power of my mind–of my *will*. Each fragment pieced seamlessly beside another, until the mirror was almost whole again. The grainier glass that had gathered itself on the carpet rose too, like dust particles in the air, clumping first before launching against the mirror and disappearing into the reflection.

I remained sitting, so much in awe and bewilderment, that I failed to notice Amy in the mirror, sitting in my father's chair again behind me.

"Well done," she praised, then stood up.

I looked at her properly. She came over to me, again brushing the hair away that had fallen over my face during my magic act.

"It really was you," she further affirmed.

"I... I did that?"

"Of course. By merely willing something, Bethany, you can make it happen."

My eyes darted from Amy to the mirror, back and forth, still unsure that I had seen what I saw. There it was, right in front of me: the mirror all repaired.

"How did it feel?"

"I don't believe it," I said.

"Oh, but others will. Trust me, Bethany. Once you harness that power and use it for what its true purpose calls, it will define you."

"What have I become?"

"You are something seldom seen in humankind," she started to explain. "Others throughout the centuries have been selected to receive the gifts you now currently possess, but only few have truly expressed the proper gratitude upon receiving them."

"Am I... like you?"

She stood over me still and turned me around so that we both were looking into the drawer-set mirror.

"No-no-no, my darling! We are worlds apart, but I think it's safe to say that we both share one common desire."

"What's that?" I asked.

"To get those who hurt you and make them suffer!"

"And, that's why you're here, isn't it? Revenge?"

"Do you think you're capable of carrying it out yourself?"

"Well, no, but I—"

"No 'buts', Bethany. You have been chosen. You hold more power than any *thing* on Earth. You could make any country leader drop dead of a heart attack right now; make the International Space Station your personal spinning toy; even consider reawakening Campi Flegrei; it's stirring from its heated slumber under Naples right now–anything you *will*. It's within you and you must use it."

"What's in it for me?"

Her eyes glistened. "Now, that's what I like to hear!"

Amy's face lit up like an excited child's. "We'll find those responsible for your… defilement, your… *pain*, and together we'll break them, torture them, and if you wish, we will kill them. All for you, Bethany Chiller, my sweet, little creation!"

We conversed the whole time by looking at one another in the mirror. Amy had placed her hands upon my shoulders, and in those moments when she got enthusiastic, she would press down on them, as if keeping me in place. Her nails like talons in their prey.

"What if I don't want to?"

"We've been through this already, haven't we? You have no choice. Besides, it'll be good for you. And think of me as your guardian… angel."

"We can't just go around killing people!"

"Why? You have all been doing it since the beginning of your creation. And don't tell me they don't deserve it."

"Of course they do," I relented.

"Go on, imagine anything. *Will* something right now: you're in possession of telekinesis; psychic abilities to listen to their fears and hear their internal screams. You rebuilt your mirror, didn't you?"

I remembered the mirror. I *rebuilt* that mirror.

"And, Bethany… they will do it again, and to another poor girl who won't have the luxury of the gifts you've been blessed with."

It was no use. She would have pursued me to the ends of the earth if I declined, especially after that terrifying initiation I endured, so I reached up to her and she took my hands in hers, which were warm and welcoming and eager.

"Tell me where to begin."

THREE

AMY designed my initial look, which was nothing special or flaunting, save for the make-up she applied. It was a bit dramatic and theatrical; I looked a bit like Melpomene, or at least a female version of that masked Muse for Tragedy. As Amy set to work, the DAB radio downstairs was belting out Pat Benatar's 1980s rock hit, *Sex As A Weapon*. She seemed to be working along with the music, styling my hair wildly, in a high, messy ponytail that cascaded from the top of my head, over my bare shoulders and halfway down my back. She instructed me to wear whatever was comfortable, so I chose my rock-inspired ripped jeans and a thick, black, polo-neck jumper.

With looks that kill and a mind that's twisted!

"There, you're all set," she said. It felt like she was mothering me.

"I want one more thing," I told her.

I reached under my pillow for the half-heart necklace that Michelle gave me; surprisingly, it was still there.

"Here," I instructed. "Put this on me."

"A talisman?" Amy enquired, interested.

"A gift, actually. A present from a friend."

"May that friendship last until the sun burns out," she said to me, and she slipped it round my neck. The thought of being garrotted didn't occur to me as she held each end of the thin chain in her hands taut across my throat. She let it relax before clipping it together at the back. The pendant slid down my jumper, resting in that smooth channel between my breasts. Amy spun me around, picking up and delicately holding the small gold heart in her hand.

"It's beautiful," she said, half-whispering, as if I weren't really meant to hear her being soft and courteous.

"It's a symbol," I said, slowly taking it from her. Had I known then Amy's true image and nature, I would have taken her words as insults. "Michelle has the other half to match mine. She's my best friend."

"I think she's closer than that," she teased.

"What do you mean?"

"She loves you. Can't you feel it?"

I thought of those private moments Michelle and I shared. To me, they weren't so sensual or provocative, no hidden meanings. Maybe sometimes Michelle was a bit forward with her feelings, but it's not like she ever tried to do anything other than offer a friendly kiss.

"I don't believe you. As a friend, yes, but we're not lovers or anything. Besides, even if we were, that would be my business, not yours."

"It's your life," Amy said, sounding disgruntled that I had rejected her idea of Michelle and I being anything other than friends. "Remember: you're no longer a virgin, Bethany."

The song finished downstairs, and there was no further music.

*****

I learned that Michelle was having a hard time dealing with the knowledge of my rape. Amy showed me how to tune into what people were doing in their lives just by concentrating on them and *willing* to see into their personal space. Total NSA-style privacy invasion, but with a supernatural twist! Of course, I didn't feel good about it, but at least there was no way I could be caught out like those spooks in 'Merica.

I tuned in to Michelle whilst she was at school; she was incredibly unsettled. She hadn't spoken to anyone about my assault, and I don't think she ever would have, but if she had confided in any of the staff, she would only be doing it to help me. I couldn't blame her.

From afar, I was satisfied that, although she was debating it furiously within herself, she wouldn't go on to reveal my ordeal to anyone. I tuned out of knowing what she was doing and thinking and brought my own consciousness back to my room.

Amy was pleased that I had invaded Michelle's thoughts.

"You'll get used to it," she said, pacing my room. "Sometimes you'll like what you learn, other times you won't. It can be a hit or a miss at times."

"If you say so," I said, rubbing my temples. I could feel an oppressing throb beginning there.

"Accept that it's part of what you are now, Bethany," Amy reminded me, looking down at me reproachfully, like I was her pupil being given a telling. "You can do things no human has ever done before!"

I sighed. Despite how crazy all of this was, she was right. Amy had taught me how to produce hot flame from my bare hands—a weapon if ever needed; had, in that short space of time, trained my telekinetic ability so that moving objects, again, by willing them to be moved, was as easy as if using my physical body to manoeuvre them. She challenged me to levitate my father's chair in the air just by looking at it, to then unwind the woven rattan fibres until they were long unbroken vines strewn across the floor and reassemble them back into the chair's original form. It seemed I had the knack for the anti-physics properties of this power.

"Come," Amy said. "It'll be dark soon, and that will be our most perfect time to strike."

"We're not just going to walk about like–"

"My dear, Bethany, have you not been watching? Just *will* it to materialise–to appear–in any place you wish. But be warned, every location has its limits and boundaries. For example, you're not capable of visiting the moon!"

"What about Heaven?"

"Heaven is an afterthought, dear girl," she snapped, angrily, though, I believe, from another time, wishfully. "It's an illusive creation from an elusive creator. It's never truly there, and neither is He."

"But you're here," I asserted. "So, that must mean it's real. All of it."

"Yes, you're right. Seeing *is* believing. But, don't you prefer the quietness, the solitude—the sanctity of the darkness?" Amy pressed for the response she was waiting to hear.

"No, not really. It freaked me out being there."

"Give it time, child. They're very welcoming."

"I don't want to know."

"Oh, but *they* do."

We continued with this back-and-forth repartee until the late evening, until I was ready to finally leave the confines of my bedroom. Amy stood by the window, looking out into the gloomy, autumn November sky. I could tell she was eager to get me outside.

"What about my mother?"

"What about her?"

"Well, I need to see her, let her know how I am, where I'm going; when I'll be back."

Amy turned around to face me. She had a smug look on her face, a kind of self-satisfied grin that beamed from ear to ear.

"You're under *my* wing now."

FOUR

THE Italian restaurant on Main Road closed its doors at 11 P.M. Illuminated by the trendy, pink glow of the halogen lights, a lone staff figure was upturning chairs and resting them upon the tables, finished for the evening. The tired waiter lifted the last of the dining chairs in the restaurant's main dining area and headed behind the bar counter to down a much-needed large glass of a customer's wasted Montepulciano d'Abruzzo.

The takings were good for the day, he was thinking, as he gulped the wine. A birthday gathering of a tough, local family had ensured that each alpha-male would be aiming to outbuy another in their rag-tag pack. Copious amounts of Dom Pérignon were consumed, running up a bill normally seen in business groups. He drained the credit from their debit cards and sent the rowdy family on their way not long ago, before commencing the routine clean-up. He had sent the other waiting staff home, and the manager, Giuseppe, was in the office in the back of the newly-refurbished building, at peace and alone with the business paperwork.

He flicked the switch to turn off the lights; the darkness began eating up the restaurant interior. The only time he had ever seen a darkness this thick was in the very early hours of the first morning of November, when he and his friends had trapped an unknown pretty girl, with each having his own way with her. They hadn't talked about it since, and for all he could see and make out from conversations in the restaurant, no one had reported it, or else in a community this small and talkative everyone would have known by now.

But he didn't feel that bad about it. Having the others there with him to carry out the attack meant he only really shouldered a quarter of the blame—of the rape. Was that what they had committed? Hell, she didn't struggle that much, so maybe she had liked it?

90

("The hell I did!")

("Keep listening, child!")

They hadn't even known who the girl was. Shaun, who was the one to suggest going to the party dressed up in the skeleton costumes, had spotted her at his school disco, and admitted when they were stunned to see her arriving at the house party that he'd love to bury his bone inside of her. The other three kept the boy at his word.

It had been pure bad luck for her that she came into the room when they were just getting high from the cannabis they'd bought. Not one of them thought himself capable of rape, but in each's drug-induced, alcohol-fuelled state, and the way that she presented herself to them in that provocative outfit...

No means no. That's what the adverts warned. Make sure it's consensual, always. By doing what? Getting them to sign a permission slip beforehand? What if they refuse to write it, or are too inebriated to do so? Well then, there'd always be forgery. And if they changed their minds halfway through, the ink will have dried by then. Boys will be boys, with their attitudes toward their toys.

Mike downed the last of the wine and turned to take the glass through to the kitchen. There, standing like a ghostly vision in front of him by the door, was a young dark-haired girl, with wild make-up and hair. Pantomime, thought Mike, quickly studying her bizarre 'mask'. This one thinks it's still fuckin' Halloween!

"How did you get in here?" he asked her, though, he couldn't see her eyes.

The girl stood still, half bathed in the smooth shadow that became like new skin over her.

"The door," she said, calmly. "You really need to make sure it stays closed. That way, nothing gets in and nothing gets out."

"Okay," Mike said, halfway between being angry at her for speaking so brazenly to him, and aroused at her shapely, unannounced appearance. She almost reminded him of...

"We're closed now, anyway," he said.

"I know. I'm not here for dinner."

"Then, what are you here for?"

"I'm here... FOR YOU!"

She raised her voice and her arms, and he felt an incredible force shove into him, like a pair of invisible hands had pushed him backwards. Hands like hers that she held outward… several feet away from him.

He stumbled and thudded back-first against the wall, breaking the glass he had been holding. A glass-paned frame holding a hygiene certificate fell to the floor.

"How… did you…?" Mike struggled to say, for he felt like his entire chest cavity had been battered. His breath escaped him, and he leaned against the wall, propping himself up with one arm.

"Do you remember me?" Bethany asked her winded assailant, though, it no longer sounded like a young female's voice. Behind it, there was something unfamiliar with more depth, more trepidation in tow.

Mike stood upright. He could envision her now: the black and red, the 69 B.C. on her outfit: the cheerleader.

"Ah, you do remember!" Bethany said, expressing her delight in her voice.

"From the party," Mike said aloud, his laboured breathing concerning him. He thought about shouting Giuseppe from the back, but it was only a girl. He could handle her.

"That's right!"

"What do you want? An apology? Another go?"

Bethany's eyes, kept hidden from him the whole time, burned like fire; Mike felt the warmth emanating from them and he looked for a direction to run. Bethany had read his mind, and before he took a step, he felt himself being dragged up the wall, like something with an immense grip had collared him from above and was lifting him by his white shirt.

Bethany stepped forward; the lights somehow came on and he could see her in full. Mike stopped thrashing and looked down at her. This was and, yet, wasn't the same girl from the party.

"P-p-please… stop…" he spluttered, unable to fully comprehend the nature of his predicament.

"You did what you wanted to me!" Bethany said aloud, for he had slid further up the wall, his head nearly butting the ceiling.

"I'm… s-s-sorry…" Mike pleaded. "I-it was the… others!"

"You all played a part," Bethany said, unequivocally.

Mike suddenly dropped to the ground, a bundle of exhaustion and fear and bewilderment. He lay for a moment, sobbing, as Bethany walked over. Her boots came into view and he started to get up. He reached out with one wavering arm, found her denim leg, and tried to pull himself up. When lifting his head to make eye contact with her, he found that those two ocular impressions remained aflame.

Delving into her newly-procured catalogue of divinity, Bethany caressed the face of her victim and recited:

"You shall not murder; and whoever murders will be liable to judgment. Everyone will be liable to judgment; until then, I say, fuck it!", and she plunged a knife straight into his throat and left it there. As he gurgled and spluttered and spat and pressed his hands around his throat, feeling around the handle of the knife, he saw a beautiful woman outside the window, dressed like a Greek goddess or an angel. Her face, illuminated by the halogenic glow, looked on, excitedly. Mike's death was imminent and with only seconds to spare, he could not help but think of something ludicrous that was both beyond and before him:

The woman was sitting on a camel.

FIVE

I knew it wasn't me; I mean, it *was* me, but the entity inside, angst-fuelled, and bloodthirsty, was in control that night.

We left the boy's body there in the restaurant, bleeding, like a burst pipe all over the smartly-tiled floor. Within an hour or so, when Amy and I retreated to the emptiness of the quarry behind my home, we heard the screaming of the emergency services' sirens as they sped to the scene of the killing. The darker part of me, my *Chiller* persona, had no interest in the ensuing conventions of the crime scene. And the knife, embedded hard and merciless in his throat like a fatal tracheotomy, would doubtless contain no trace of my DNA, for Hell has a way of erasing its tracks and ensuring the anonymity of any of its own.

"How did it feel?" Amy asked, walking alongside me on the uneven rocky ground.

I didn't come to until we ended up skulking in the quarry; my internal other half kept within the confines of my skin a little longer than I would have liked, revelling in her newfound position as my alter ego. When I found my head again, I was forcibly sick.

"It was disgusting!" I said. "You said we weren't going to kill."

"No, I said we would torture and *maybe* kill them–it was you who did the killing!"

I tried to oppose her, but she was evading responsibility like church.

"You *used* me to do it!"

"Not true; I didn't give you the knife, only the power and reasoning to carry out what you really aim to do."

"I can still go to the police," I said, "they'll take a statement, and after tonight maybe the others will confess."

Amy looked down her nose at me. She always could and would, for she was and acted like my superior.

"Don't you think your law enforcement will be a little suspicious that one of your attackers has now ended up with a blade in his throat? That someone may have wished each of them dead?"

I looked up at the stars. A clear, cloudless sky. I blew out the air in my lungs to try feel more at peace, settle my nerves.

"Okay, you win, Amy," I conceded. "You've got it all worked out."

"They didn't rape *me*, child," Amy said. "They deserve this, Bethany–that useless waste of flesh and blood got his."

"I don't feel too good," I moaned, genuinely. My head hurt and so did my stomach, from the vomiting. I was sure I'd also torn my throat whilst retching.

"Perhaps we should get you home, then," she said to me, a considerate offer.

"Perhaps we should," I said irreverently, though, it was not lost on her. She narrowed her eyes, an acknowledgement of my nippy retort.

Although the house was only several feet away, I closed my eyes and imagined my bedroom. Within seconds I was there.

*****

Amy favoured sitting in my father's wicker chair more than any other place in my room. Sometimes it bothered me to see her sitting in it, all relaxed and sweet-as-icing, knowing what she was.

We had both transported into the room; I was still piecing together fragments of the scene at the restaurant whilst Amy studied me from the chair. Outside, a couple more flashing blue lights lit up the street as their vehicles flew past. Local social media would be blowing up about the incident.

"They can't trace you," Amy said, apparently reading my

mind.

I was sat on the bed. My tabby cat had been in the room with us, at ease upon the covers; when we materialised in the room she looked up and saw us but didn't care much.

"The police?" I asked, already knowing.

"It's been dealt with. It's as if you were never there."

I felt somewhat relaxed.

"What's next?"

"That's up to you, Bethany. One down, three to go!"

"We're not killing again."

"That's up to you, too," Amy said, as if it were truly my choice. "If it were up to me, they would all be burning in Hell right now. But, as it happens, it's what *you* want to do. I must support that."

"Like fuck you do!"

Amy was taken aback by my snappy outburst. She hadn't expected a little attitude after the night we just had.

"What do you mean?" asked Amy, leaning forward, inquisitively.

"You are only here for yourself."

"That's a bit self-referential; you needed me, and I came. Why do you say that?"

"Because it's what you do! That's why you didn't stop it! You sit and watch while all this goes on!"

"It is my area of expertise," Amy said, coolly. "But the rest of it's not my department, Bethany. I'm afraid there are higher powers that set the stage. We're just the performance."

"This isn't theatre," I said, and with that, that line of conversation ended.

We sat quietly for a few minutes, before I decided to get up and remove the make-up from my face. I sat by the drawer set and gazed longingly in the mirror. I pulled forth my wild hair, lengthening the single ponytail out over my shoulders and down my front. What had Amy made me into? What had I become?

She appeared behind me, a darling vision.

"I'm sorry, Bethany, I just want what's best for you."

She slipped her arms around me, comforting me, for she had noticed the tears in my eyes.

"I know all of this is not easy to take in," she said. "You are incredibly young, and reluctantly religiously ignorant. But I only want to help you and see that justice is delivered."

Through my teary vision I looked at her in the mirror. Her head, near mine; her chin resting upon my shoulder. As she spoke, her jaw vibrated on the bone.

"Tomorrow night," said Amy, "we'll get another. And if you don't want to kill him, I promise to intervene if you're going too far."

"You'll intervene?" I asked, sounding mockingly shocked.

"For you," she whispered, kissing me on the cheek.

Then, she was gone, and it was just me and my cat. Her jade eyes, curious to learn how this other womanly figure could appear and disappear like that, were glistening, as if the cat itself could feel my despair.

SIX

I was restless that night. I tried everything I could think of to get to sleep, but all I kept seeing were visions of that earlier evening, when Mike had met his (deserved) gruesome end.

The knife, sticking out of his throat like a lever whilst his blood leaked out from the wound, was a phallic symbol representing what he and his cohorts had done to me.

They stuck something in me, so I returned the favour.

It was now Wednesday morning, 3rd November; I'd dreamt about my dad again, which was actually a lot like the first dream I had when he appeared. Again, that light called to him and pulled him back just as he was in the process of warning me again. I woke up thinking I had to try harder to communicate with him should he re-visit.

There's a field nearby that's already been used by the locals to build a fire for the forthcoming Bonfire Night. Old and broken items of furniture were stacked à la *Tetris*, connecting and creating such a sublime structure that it bordered on perfection. It was a neat pre-lit stack that was set to get bigger and bulkier.

I thought it best to return to school this morning. I had to return to some degree of normalcy, no matter how hard it seemed. No matter what had gone on in the last few days, I was still a sixteen-year old girl.

*****

As I walked out of my garden gate and down the road, I looked at Graeme's house. No curtain-twitching at this time of the morning. I had thought about stealing into his mind and gather some truths about him and his person, but like

Amy had warned me, there were some things I wouldn't like to learn.

Another drizzly, cold morning greeted me on my walk; lost in my own thoughts, I tried to take no notice of the puddles under me or the dull-grey sky that hung above. I just wanted to get to school, try catch up with Michelle and let her see how I was doing.

By mid-morning, just when I thought I had settled back in, something startling happened in art class. We had finished working on some informal appreciation of René Magritte, the Belgian master surrealist, and I was about ready to begin something on the canvas that was inspired by *The Lovers* oil painting, when I heard Amy speaking to me in my head.

Go to her.

Who? I answered.

Michelle. Your friend.

And suddenly, the page in the art book on my table that displayed Magritte's 1928 classic, changed before my eyes. The characters' veiled profiles individually morphed so that my face was that of the woman dressed in red, with my head submissively positioned upwards; my embrace with Michelle, my black-suited partner, unveiled, exposed. There was that Taoist symbol again, staring me in the face. Or, was this Amy's concoction? Trying to expand on her guesswork that Michelle was in love with me by manipulating the things around me? Or, perhaps this image was being relayed from my very own confused heart?

Without freaking, I closed the book, hurriedly excused myself, and left the class to go to the bathroom. I headed straight for the girls' toilets at the end of the long, empty corridor, relieved to find no-one else in sight. The toilets were empty, too. I entered a cubicle and closed the door behind me. The smell of disinfectant was almost overpowering; I sat after laying down the lid, giddy and slightly nauseas. Then, the school bell rang; it was the end of period three: break-time. As expected, a chorus of clicking heels and thudding flat shoes soon trampled in, with high-pitched voices and laughter above those. I recognised one of the voices that was chirping away like a little excited bird.

"Did it really happen?" a girl said.

"I think so, but no one's seen her yet to ask," was the disembodied reply, whom I expected belonged to Lisa, my personal party invitation.

I sat on the toilet seat, eager to learn more about what the girls were discussing. My first thought was that it was about me. I could have entered each of their minds and got the information I wanted, but on this occasion, without Amy by my side, I refrained from doing that.

"I got told she took on more than one," another voice added. I was certain there were at least three of them out there.

"Well, let's just leave a little message here," a voice spoke that was definitely Lisa's.

I heard a smudging sound, and I suspected they were writing something on the mirror above the washbasin. When the message was finished, the author capped her writing implement and all the girls left the room.

After a few moments of waiting to see if any would return, I unlocked the door and read the vile message daubed on the mirror in what appeared to be red lipstick (why's it always in red?):

BETHANY C. GOT GANG-BANGED!

It was a brutal reminder of my torment. But, how had they known about it? Someone obviously had talked. I knew it hadn't been Michelle, so it was likely after Mike's murder that someone said something, probably one of the other three. I would wait and converse with Amy later, to see what she knew. I grabbed some paper towels, wrapped them around my hand and wiped away the words on the glass.

No one had to see this. No one else had to know.

SEVEN

I managed to psychically find where Michelle was. Although we were in the same year, we had different classes. Only P.E. and Business Studies we shared.

I got hold of her as she exited the Science building. She looked the worse for wear (I learned she hadn't been sleeping well) and when she saw me approaching her, she later admitted she had been in two minds as to whether she should acknowledge me or avoid me.

"Hey," I said first, directly in front of her. "Where have you been?"

"Bethany, why are you back at school so soon?"

"I can't hide away forever," I said.

"I take it you've heard about the murder at the restaurant," she asked, rarely looking me in the eye.

"Yeah, weird, eh?"

"Too many terrible things are happening around here lately; I don't suppose you've been to the police, yet? I could come with you."

"Don't worry, it's all worked out."

"How do you mean?" Michelle asked.

"It's all being taking care of. Those guys don't know what's coming."

"Bethany…" Michelle said, with a slight pause, "…you're scaring me."

"Not as much as they'll be when I'm done."

She reached out to caress my arm.

"We need to get you help and support, Bethany. I'm worried that you're still in some state of shock."

I appreciated her genuine concern for me but knowing then

what I did and what I was capable of I had to refuse Michelle's willingness to support me. Even if I told her the whole truth, I didn't think she would be able to handle it any better than I was. I could have shown her something unnatural, thereby forcing her to believe me, but that wouldn't be fair, would it? What right did I have in forcing her to bear witness to something she couldn't explain logically, naturally? That wasn't my area of expertise; as Amy professed, 'higher powers' were in charge.

"Well, I'm coping fine, Michelle. But, thanks for everything. You know, you don't need to keep away."

"I'm not keeping away, Bethany. I'm just giving you some space, letting *you* decide when you want to talk."

I knew that was mostly true. She felt for me, for definite.

"Why don't you come 'round this evening," I suggested.

"Yeah, sure; I'll drop by around seven, if that's good for you?"

"It should be fine. Okay, see you then."

We hugged before heading off to our next class. With any luck, Amy wouldn't be around when Michelle came to visit.

*****

"So, that's how we're doing it?"

I was growing angry at Amy's repeated, casual reappearances in my room. I knew she was watching me daily, all day, and while I didn't expect to see any warning signs when she decided to show, I would have preferred it if she found a way to announce it beforehand. I'd then be able to properly compose myself whilst awaiting the privilege of her company.

"I didn't think you would mind, Bethany." Again, sat in the wicker chair.

"But we don't need to rush this, do we?"

She sat up quickly; motivated. "They are getting away with what they did to you! Every second you allow them to breathe, they're revelling in how they *took* you, one by one, and how you did *nothing* to fight back!"

I saw the phosphorescent bones of their jumpsuits flash before my eyes. Amy was really forcing it through to make her point.

"Hey, I know what they did to me! I *was* there!"

Amy sat back in the chair. I heard it creaking under the pressure of her, but it would hold her svelte figure. That time I took it apart using my mind and rebuilt it must have made it less sturdy. But that's what happens when you take something apart, right? It never seems to fit back together the way it did. And it's not that there's anything missing–it's just the parts have changed, mutated, become *something else* entirely.

"Just don't forget why I'm here," she said, a bitter-sweet reminder.

"I can't forget. I won't let me."

She got up from the chair and stood in front of the mirror. She seemed pleased with herself, how she looked, how she dressed. I suppose, if I had a body like hers as a full-grown woman–that hour-glass, serpentine figure–I'd be pleased, too.

"Haven't you learned how old I am?" Amy asked, rhetorically. It was impossible for me to even guess, let alone know, her true age.

"You know I don't know," I said. "But, from all that you've told me, you're pretty old!"

She ignored my joke, instead focusing on her reflection. She turned this way and that, studying her body with a critical eye.

"Most men fall for me when they see this. They immediately lose interest in everything else in their lives for that short duration I own them."

I had not the time nor the interest in listening to her self-obsessed ramblings. Sure, she was helping me, but on whatever personal crusade she rode on into my life, I had no business derailing her. She was a stubborn, determined demon (aren't they all?). So, I figured I'd better feign interest.

"Then what do you do with them?" I asked.

"I use and abuse them, child!" She laughed right after this, and I believed her. With a reserved hatred, I instilled belief in her acumen.

It was nearing seven. Amy knew Michelle was on her way; she had psychically wire-tapped her way into our conversation at school earlier.

"Shall we go before your girlfriend arrives?"

I finished dressing that way she liked me to (jeans, boots and jacket, with that wild ponytail she helped brush–I looked like *Jessica Jones*).

"I always ask, do I have a choice?"

"Yes, you do, and no, you don't. My time on Earth to help you is not unlimited, Bethany. I do have other places I can be; other souls to guide."

"So, am I to be used and abused, too, Amy?" I said, angrily, confrontationally, as I put on my jacket.

Amy walked over and took hold of the zip just as I prepared to pull it up. She gripped my hand, but in a non-violent way.

"Never."

With ease she ran the zipper up, stopping at my chest. She then placed her hand over my gold half-heart and closed her eyes. She was finding pleasure in this.

"So much power remains," she whispered. "In the pieces of a broken heart."

She could have been talking about either of them.

I left a note for Michelle on my drawer-set letting her know I wouldn't be long, as I knew she would be invited in. I hated absconding from the house, but there was no way I could let my mother know what was going on. It was a wonder she hadn't walked in on us already!

We were heading to a theme park, one of the country's biggest and best. Although as the crow flies, the journey should have been miles, we got there by simply willing ourselves there. Amy ensured that we appeared in the wooded area that surrounded the park, so we wouldn't be exposed. She gave me strict instructions on what I was to do, where I was to go, whilst she remained on the outside, 'listening'. She would join me when it was time.

I looked at the entrance to the theme park. There was a queue almost out the door; the remaining Halloween shows were on their way out, but for those who missed them at the weekend, the park was running them again this last week before they scuttled off into hiding until next year, where they would resurface, new and improved.

The bright advertising boards for these events stood outside. Zombie attractions, haunted rooms and park rides—this seemed like my kind of place. And tonight, it definitely was:

One of my attackers was in there.

EIGHT

At the booth, I bought a ticket to the zombie event, which was a well-decorated, closed-in run-around maze designed to have you experience–and run from–an undead outbreak. It sounded loud and menacing. Lots of screaming, laughter, and other theatrical effects booming outside had the people in the queue fearing.

I waited nervously in line; someone behind me had set off some party poppers which made me jump with fright every time one went off. I watched a young child nearby work a machine that could catch toys in a claw and drop them as prizes, but this little boy was having no luck. I decided to help.

As he worked the control sticks to move the claw device inside the Plexiglass box, he managed to grab a small Frankenstein in the mountain of Halloween toys. As the claw withdrew from this monster-summit, barely gripping the soft toy; it swung about on its flexible fixing, a shady attempt to 'drop' the item back into the mix. I gazed steely at the finger-like appendages of the machine and willed them to remain tight. I suppose I could have been doing this for nothing and it was all down to the mechanics of the machine, but when the claw came to a stop and prepared to release the toy for the drop hatch, it didn't do anything. It hovered teasingly above it, with the miniature Frankenstein swaying in its thin, metal fingers. I touched the Plexiglass and got a static shock from it whilst I attempted to psychically manipulate the machine.

The claw vibrated, a slight tremor along its structure that signalled to me I had something to do with it. The boy was watching my hand–I think he thought I was going to find a way in and get the toy.

"Don't worry," I told him, looking down at his upset face. "I'll get it out for you."

I focused my attention back onto the claw, still with my palm against the machine. I was mentally saying *Drop! drop!* whilst pressing lightly onto the Plexiglass. Then, suddenly, the claw sprung open, all three of its spindly fingers springing outward and releasing little Frankie into the hatch.

The boy squealed in delight. He retrieved the toy and showed it to me.

"I can't share this with you, but thanks," he said, politely.

I remember thinking what a charming, observant child he was. Moments later, he ran off into a sea of people. I hoped he would keep the toy for a while, as a reminder of what this wild-haired, biker-looking-chick had done for him.

The chatter going on inside the foyer in no way drowned out the screams and shouts heard coming from the enclosure I was queueing to get into. The line was shortening much quicker, as the staff were inviting in enlarged groups of up to ten every ten minutes or so.

Then, I saw him.

I had a knot in my stomach the moment I caught sight of him; he had his arm casually around a young woman as they stood at the head of the queue. If the head count was as I expected, I'd be in the same group as him.

*****

I felt stupid whilst waiting in that line that night. Here was one of my rapists–the one who guarded the bedroom door–standing all smug with his attractive tart, waiting to experience the latest, scariest event in the theme park, and I, mere metres from him, patiently waiting to deliver the same! I mean, Amy would be tearing her hair out at the thought!

The blackened entrance to the horror attraction swallowed up the few bodies at the end of the line; I kept my head down and, not desperate to make eye contact with anyone, shuffled forward until I was standing in a small group. A staff member took my ticket as I slouched behind a big, long-haired guy in a denim jacket. Again, the sights and sounds of the horror event bounded around us and the nervous and anxious alike wailed.

I felt my gut knotting again, tightening in a cramp, but I also sensed excitement, anticipation, building, knowing what was about to happen.

The staff member quickly ran us through the procedure, the dos and don'ts of the activity.

"And please don't hit out at the performers!" he said. "They *will* hit back!"

And thus, they were warned.

NINE

I met with Amy inside. She had called to me telepathically and I sought her presence in the presiding darkness of the tunnel through which we were encouraged to hurry along. In among the blinding lights, impressive, scary theatrics, and speakers booming horror audio in quality surround sound, I managed to keep up with my attacker.

Amy knew exactly what he looked like, and so after he rushed past with his woman, I stood at the threshold of a brick alcove that curved just above my head, and Amy peeled out of that black arch unexceptionally, as if there had been an invisible door opened to let her out.

"You know which one it is?"

I nodded, suddenly burning with an intensity to proceed. I didn't want them ending the experience and getting away. I wanted to trap the fucker in here–with me.

"Go to him, child," she instructed, half remaining in the unnatural extended blackness of the alcove. "And ensure that he knows who you are!"

She fell back into the shadows whilst I moved on. I could feel another power taking over me; a forceful, rushing sensation that I could not fight. In fact, in this moment, I wanted it to take over.

The group that I had merged into were now herded together in a room that was decorated and designed like a bomb shelter, complete with fake, corrugated iron roof and steel walls. Hazard warning trefoil posters had been put up: biological hazards, ionising radiation, generic caution–pretty much the advertisement for a nuclear party gone wrong. Posters were piled in the corner, unkempt, to indicate the hectic, hurried pace that the poster-hangers in this fictional world's shelter would have found themselves in. Obviously, the situation had fast went south. Fake blood was splattered all over the place, as well as impressive fake body parts dispersed over the floor. This survival-fraught party-room had fast become an eatery.

A loudspeaker in the top corner of the shelter crackled and buzzed to life. Feedback squealed in the air around us for a few moments before shrieking away. Then, a man's voice sounded from the loudspeaker, echoing tinny in our small space.

"Attention, survivors!" his voice called. "If you're hearing me then good! We haven't lost you yet!"

It was inspiring to bear witness to respectful, copycat effects from most every zombie flick being played out. The main door to the shelter slammed shut, and the loudspeaker imitated the sound of the door being bolted from the other side, to add to the already-heightened tension within. The denim jacket-wearing guy, who was relishing the whole episode unreservedly, pulled at the handle. The door was, indeed, locked.

"Again, if anyone is hearing this, I need you… before… seventy-two hours…"

The voice was patchy, erratically breaking at key parts and coming through hisses of static. The tone and speed of the announcer was wild and rushed, as if he were trapped in his own shelter of sorts. In his background, banging sounds could be heard, as if an undead horde pounded incessantly on his door.

I caught my attacker whispering something to his companion, which made her laugh. Oh! if only she knew what he was *really* like.

The lights went out in the shelter; we were about halfway through the course. The other group members with me started freaking out, but not in a serious way (they all assumed it was part of the experience). Then, on the outside, there began hammering upon the door, fists and boots trying to bash their way in to reach us. And in the centre of the floor, beside a blood-splattered desk, a pillar of flame shot upward and struck the fake roof but did not set it alight. Everyone thought it was cool special effects; I knew it was Amy, letting me know she was in here, too.

I experienced dizziness that caused my consciousness to evaporate; I felt like I was about to faint, but not entirely. It was like being stuck in a revolving door, and the entity about to exit on the half turn was her, *Bethany Chiller*. With all self-control gone I was, once more, lost and wandering within myself.

✸✸✸✸✸

The sudden upward burst of fire hadn't burned anyone, some swift pyrotechnic setup designed to frighten the group whose turn it now was to be stuck in the shelter. Having the lights go off didn't seem to help things, either, but in total, the experience thus far was worth the admission price.

There was a big guy in a denim jacket who went over to the try the door, but it was locked. And although the lights were out, some natural light from outside had filtered into the shelter, and every member of the group, each in their own distressed state (albeit pretend), stood uncomfortably in the darkness, unaware of what to do amidst the thumping that went on the outer side of the door.

"This is intense!" someone called out. One or two others agreed.

The loudspeaker had gone silent; someone asked what they should do next, but no-one really had an answer. In the darkness, the group shuffled around, felt for things around them: papers, bookshelves, writing implements. It was still light enough to ensure that no-one could get themselves hurt, despite all the scare elements with the fake fire and the door-hammering.

There was a girl watching him, Shaun detected. Did she look familiar? She did, a bit. The hair, blacker in this blackness, was a giveaway. He had seen that much of it on someone else recently…

He didn't pay it any more mind, instead, became embroiled in the group's get-together, which was scrambling to form ideas on how to combat the unsettling situation they were in.

"We could try forcing the door?" someone suggested.

"*It's really heavy. It probably won't budge—and it's locked!*" came a reply.

"*Well, there is a way out of here somehow!*"

"*What about that flame?*" someone got excited at saying.

"*What about it?*"

"*Well, it had to come from somewhere!*"

"*I doubt it's a way out.*"

Shaun offered to ram the door. The others, though quietly concluding it would make no massive dent in their situation, gave him the thumbs-up to at least try. They thought his plan was a bit intense, but something had to be done.

He separated from them, geared himself up mentally, and got into position to shoulder-barge the heavy door, on which the banging had ceased. Bethany glared at him in the darkness as he prepared to sprint. She watched the dumb fuck run like a mindless bull against the door; the impact shook the walls around them, and just as the group had secretly surmised, the door didn't budge.

Shaun returned to his beau, dejected, and slightly embarrassed. She smiled to let him know it was okay that he didn't succeed. He then locked eyes with Bethany, and she knew he recognised her.

Shaun started to get all flustered; nothing too maniacal, but enough to startle his companion. Bethany could feel the intensity building, her blood rushing; her teeth growing into fangs that could rip flesh, nails extending to claws that could tear metal. The demonic spirit was emerging, transforming her into a creature of no earthly origin. And, as Bethany wandered alone, Godless and confused, in the recesses of her mind, unable to prevent Amy's creation from becoming, she could sense this entity's anticipation, its excitement, her power that they both shared.

Another flame erupted from the same spot as before, and in this bright, fiery light, Shaun could see the monster across the room from him. It was the girl from the party, and yet, it wasn't. It was hideous. Monstrous. And standing behind her, there was another female: taller, a bit more human, but with the same black lifeless eyes; and something that sparkled around her waist. Shaun had not seen this figure in the group before.

The group jumped with fright and began shouting for help at the unexpected burst of flame; they started to pound on the door for its release as the bunker-like space filled with smoke.

"What's on fire?" someone shouted.

"For fuck's sake, find it and put it out!"

"We can't see anything in here!"

And it was true. The darkness had increased, and the group's banging provided the creature with the perfect distraction. She lunged forward and pulled Shaun away from his girlfriend, almost tearing his arm from its socket; he called out in confusion and fear but knew deep down just who it was that had him in her grasp.

Together, they collapsed into the corner, and the black there swallowed them both.

The lights came back on. There was no trace of smoke or fire.

And there were two missing from their party.

*****

They were, again, surrounded by darkness, in a void that was once created by the mind of God, and given its damned identity by the Devil. The girl, with the face of a twisted demon, continued to hold her prisoner—her victim—in a chokehold. He could feel her breath on his neck; could imagine her puncturing his jugular with those damn fangs…

She let him go, and he stumbled before he landed on the groundless black floor. Was it glass flooring? Walls? Were they simply floating? He didn't feel like he was weightless. Then what the hell were they standing on?

"It's exactly what you're standing on," the girl-creature spoke to him.

"Huh?"

"Hell, you piece of shit! It's but a short drop below you," she explained. "But first I need to know that you know why I've brought you here."

"I… we… not in Hell…" he stuttered much whilst taking in the utterly viewless scenery around him.

"Please," he commenced pleading, "let me go! Take me back—I won't say anything to anyone."

The girl with the wild black hair, leather jacket and unholy creature-face, laughed at his request.

"You have no idea, don't you?" she said. "You know me, but you're unwilling to remember me. Or what you and the others did."

"The others?"

"Mike's already been taken care of," she taunted, "and the rest of you will follow suit."

The revelation hit him fully. She was the girl from the Halloween party: the one they had raped.

"Oh, my god! It is you! Please, I am so, so sorry about that night! It wasn't my idea; if I could, I'd take it back! We'd never hurt anyone again like that!"

The girl stepped closer, treading upon what was groundless black space.

"That's why I'm here, Shaun, to ensure it never happens again."

"Did you kill Mike?"

"With ease."

"Please, don't kill me! What would you like me to do? Go to the police? I'll admit my crime! I swear it! I'll tell them what we did to you… you…"

But Bethany Chiller had no interest in his repentance, or his selfishness. Another entity would be responsible for this mortal's redemption. What was done was done, and it was down to her to mete out justice: judge, jury, jailor.

Then, trotting out of the blackness to his left, appeared the woman whom he had seen standing behind the girl whilst in the room—she was riding upon a camel. He could tell by the non-saddled hump.

"He's yours, Bethany!" said the camel-riding woman to the girl.

She urged the ungulate beast onward with a thump to its side.

Shaun's stomach felt as if it was about to give way. The mixture of fear and confusion and paranoia ate away at his insides; his guts swirled and churned like the ice pellets in a slushy drink machine.

The girl, whom he now knew as Bethany, demanded he fall to his knees. Looking down, the blackness of the invisible ground on which they stood appeared to fall forever. It was a wonder they were even stable and standing at all.

He knelt slowly before Bethany; she stood before him and placed her hand on his head once he was still. The burning sensation that had begun emanating from her palms suddenly intensified; his scalp cooked, and his hair singed from the flames that flew from her palms. He screamed out at her to stop, but she held him now with two fiery, red-hot hands. He grabbed at her wrists; she remembered him doing that in the bedroom *when he held her down for the others. The bruises had remained on her feminine skin. The fiery heat travelled down her arms and through his own hands; they became raw and the skin softened so that it began melting before he had to let go.*

His face reddened as his screaming increased; it bulged and pulsated as wave after wave of searing heat tore through his skull. His nostrils and ears leaked blood, just as his tongue sizzled and burned up in his mouth, and his eyeballs blasted violently out of their sockets in a splatter of blood vessels and mucus membrane.

Moments later, his dead body, skull-fried-black with charred flesh and remnants of hair and eye in between her fingers, limped in her grasp. She dropped the lifeless lump to the invisible ground, before it was swallowed into an even more undistinguishable black hole and out of view entirely.

Amy, atop her ride, clapped at the deadly performance.

"See? It's getting easier now. Perfectly done! The fruits of fear and pain bear an indelible aftertaste, wouldn't you agree?"

Bethany Chiller sneered at her recent kill, and then grinned at her mistress's appreciation and praise. She indulged in the admiration.

They both did.

TEN

THERE was no immediate need to return to the theme park; I wouldn't be shown on the closed-circuit cameras, anyway, and they would have just listed Shaun as missing. The police would have to deal with that problem, like they were with Mike's.

So, two down, two to go, right? You must be thinking that I enjoyed those double killings? You couldn't be any further from the truth! Sure, those bastards got their comeuppance, but at what price? An eye for an eye? Tooth for a tooth? Two wrongs do not make a right. Not even four of 'em.

But Amy made me feel like they were. She convinced me that, although under that dreadful, demonic influence, my revenge was justified. Would a court of law agree? Would God?

We arrived back in my bedroom; Michelle had been 'round, for she had written it below the text on the note I had left for her.

"Oh, we missed your friend?" Amy said, reading the note.

I snatched it out of her hands. It was my private correspondence, not hers.

"Never mind that! You told me there would be no more killing!"

With a dramatic pout, Amy disagreed with me.

"No, I said I'd intervene if I thought you were going too far."

"Then, why didn't you?"

"Well," she started briefly, "I didn't think you went far enough."

Exasperated, I faced away from her, my hands on my hips,

making me look like a humanoid, double-handled pot of some kind, like something out of *Beauty and the Beast*. I was irate.

"*Far enough*? Another boy is *dead*, Amy! Murdered!"

"Nobody will ever know it was you, Beth—"

"*I* will know, Amy! *Me*, Bethany…"

I struggled at that point to remember my original surname.

I sat myself down on the wicker chair, whilst Amy knelt upon my bed. Her pose, there: provocative, alluring, *deliberate*.

"I thought… I thought that you were sent to *help* me…"

"I was, and I *am*," said Amy.

I was shaking; tears were welling up behind my tired eyes, and as I struggled to contain them, I witnessed flashes of the hellish murder of Shaun in my mind. Those mental photography snippets, breaking out of my memory like an illegal transmission. Only, these were mostly grainy images— not like the visual noise from your typical TV—dotted intermittently with flesh and flame.

Amy shifted from being on her knees to sitting on the edge of the bed facing me. Her legs were together, prim and proper, and she regarded me as if *she* were the one who had the right to ask the questions.

"Don't you feel I'm helping?"

"No, not really."

"But the power I've given you? The things you know—"

"They don't mean anything to me. Not really. I mean, what does a sixteen-year old girl want to do with power like this, anyway? Other than exact revenge on evildoers…"

I trailed off because sleep had a hold on me.

"And, is that not fulfilling for you?"

"Amy," I began, sleepily, "it's all a fantasy, isn't it? The magic, the terror—it's all make-believe."

She was offended. The look on her face; a combination of hard, glaring eyes and bared, clenched teeth.

"Witch! There is nothing *pretend* about who I am, what I do, or where I'm from. Consider yourself lucky not to have had any one of Hell's darkest numbers accost you in the way I have! They would have mauled you worse than those boys just to teach you a lesson! Take it from me, child: you're safer in my arms."

I wasn't caring that she was spouting off yet another mystic speech about her fabled origins; I was nearly asleep, and hopefully, of another chance to meet my dad in it.

I was in luck. Amy saw that I was snoozing and whilst angry and annoyed, she disappeared entirely in a lick of eerie flame that could not singe neither man nor beast.

*****

My dad, arriving with the heavenly light to steal a few moments with his daughter in her deep dream state, approached me. I felt nothing but love for him. And loss. *For Me.*

"She nearly has you, Bethany," he began, like a loud whisper that seemed to reverberate all around my head. "But do not fear her; she cannot harm you."

"But, dad, I've gone on to do terrible things," I admitted, though, he would already have known.

He hugged me; it felt the same as it always had. *My father.*

He pulled away, his touch so real. His arms, so big and welcoming.

"You are being watched over," my dad said, with hope and delight in his eyes. "You feel that light back there? Well, it's not just my taxi, you know!"

Even in the afterlife, he still made me laugh by being as funny as ever. *My father.*

"Well, there are things in that light that can overpower and even overrule anything else that's in or out of the world."

Now it was my turn to have hope in my sight.

"You're not wholly responsible for… things… and the light knows this," he revealed. "You must try to resist her full agenda right until the end. Don't manifest your desire to punish those who hurt you, Bethany."

"Is that what I really want, daddy?" I asked honestly of him, for I didn't entirely know myself my own true reasons.

"Revenge? Justice, baby, will be carried out in time. It's not up to us to decide when. Like it wasn't up to me when I passed aw—"

The light called to him, then. Without a voice, it *called* to him. *My father.*

I tried to hold onto his arm as he apologised and walked backward and away from me. But, as he retreated, he never took his eyes off me. And before the light embraced him, he blew me a kiss that I knew I felt sweep across my cheek, losing absolutely no substance through the air from his palm.

In seconds, he was gone again. My inspiration, my hero.

My father.

ELEVEN

I awoke with a start. It was Thursday morning, 4th November.

My cat was curled up at the bottom of my bed. Nothing new there. I wasn't sure whether or not to attend school that day; I thought I'd skip the morning, at least, maybe go for a walk and try to clear my head.

I was still in my clothes from the excursion the night before, so I thudded down the stairs and headed for the front door.

"Bethany!"

My mum was home. She was in the kitchen, eating breakfast. I hungered so much; I hadn't been looking after myself that well that week. In fact, I don't think I had eaten or drank anything proper since the weekend.

"Bethany!" she called again, desperate for my attention and answer. "I haven't seen you properly for days, Bethany. Are you still speaking to me?"

I opened the front door.

"Course."

I wasn't aiming to be horrible to her; I just needed a bit of fresh air and something to jumpstart my being that morning. The dream of my father had shaken me up, and the boy's death from the night before weighed unbelievable heavy on my mind.

"Well, good, because I've missed you—"

The sound of the door slamming shut cut her off. I felt like shit doing that to her—my own mother. But she would never have understood any of what was happening to me. As far as she knew, I was suffering with mega period pains, stomach cramps, and other lovely lady-problems.

I walked in the opposite direction to Michelle's house, even though at this time, I knew she would be in school. I also had 'tuned in' to her (a process in which I had to think only of her and like a spiritual GPS, her location was revealed); I also sensed she was feeling angry and hurt about missing me last night (another benefit of these powers). She felt like I was avoiding her or playing stupid games by not taking my predicament as seriously as she thought I should. I would have to work hard at repairing everything in our friendship, or I would risk losing it and damage her forever.

Graeme, that ex-postie-turned-curtain-twitcher, was watching me. Not from his favourite window—from across the street. He walked at the same pace as I did. I kept my head down, away from the creep, but he pursued me from the other side.

Then, he crossed the road.

I wanted no part of it. I knew he was heading for me, and of course, I knew about the things he was doing at home (the photographs, the masturbation). As soon as he stepped onto the road and took a few steps, I stared at him and he stopped bang in the middle, instantly puzzled. Why? Because I had willed it.

He looked down at his shoes, as if they had betrayed him and were now glued to the tarmac. He frustratingly pulled at his legs, tying to move each onward, but his determination was no match for mine.

A car was fast approaching. Like a sitting duck—except, this foul waterfowl was terrifyingly aware—the Zafira speeding along was in no position to brake in time, because I was willing that, too.

Graeme looked up at me, puzzled and with abashed fright; and I think he suspected I was holding some influence over him.

There really is no spectacular version of events that occurred swiftly after; the black Zafira smashed into the pervert, killing him instantly and only minorly injuring the driver and cracking the windshield. No one else was around to witness Graeme's death, and I ensured the driver was unable to see me the whole time.

In a way, I feel remorse because the man had done nothing wrong to me. But what if he had been about to? Considering what I told you about the things I knew about him 'off the record', he may very well have had something sinister in mind when he took those fateful steps toward me that morning.

I guess we'll never know now. Shame.

TWELVE

TIME was running out. I could feel this foreboding presence clawing at me, at my heart, that all the good things that had once been in me were being savagely eaten by this demonic presence in my body. It was something that my dad had said in that last dream, about not succumbing to Amy's agenda, and to resist it until the end. At the time, I had no idea what he meant, but I of course, do now.

With two down (plus one) and two still to go, I continued my walk that morning. I had no reason to call for help after Graeme's road accident; adjudicators in the afterlife would deal with him, I knew.

It was also unbelievably hard to concentrate; I could hear hawkish whisperings, disembodied voices chanting through the air as I walked. At times, a fleeting shadow; others, a full, black-bodied entity there one second, then slipping into the shadows the next. My eyes were wide and my consciousness on full alert to these devilish beings that were on the prowl, following me. For what and why would just be me speculating; they could know at any time where I was and what I was doing, so I didn't understand the need for being tailed.

The police presence in the town had noticeably increased. I sensed that some folk were still living with unease over Mike's brutal killing in the restaurant; if I could, I'd assure the locals that they had nothing to worry about.

I came to a park that had a couple of little children playing in. I sat on a nearby bench to catch my breath and regain my composure. The sky remained dull and uninspiring, the ground wet and unappealing. If I wanted, I could have it opened and swallowing every living thing nearby, sending it all into that black pit: Hell. Despite initiating that third killing, I didn't harbour feelings of wilful death and destruction.

I must have been on that hard bench, reigning in the most monstrous thoughts and images, for around half an hour when alarm bells began ringing in my mind. I did feel that something in the 'world' wasn't right, that somewhere nearby there was an event happening that warranted my attention and, if need be, my intervention. Using my mind, I was able to track and zone in on the conversation that was about to ensue. It was my worst fear.

Amy had found Michelle.

*****

The demon finally caught up with my best friend in the school canteen; decorations for Bonfire Night had begun, and parodies of Guy Fawkes were being pinned or hung up in the dining area that morning. Posters of the dangers of fireworks–as well as advertising their beautiful displays–were tacked along the walls.

Michelle was sitting on her own, eating lunch, when an unfamiliar woman approached her at the table (I want you to note Amy's appearance here: her above-the-knee, black pencil skirt, killer heels; her hair in a bun, and her blouse unbuttoned one or two buttons too much, depending on how liberal or conservative you were–but, her face remained the same). Was this satanic bitch trying to impress or flirt with my friend?

"Michelle Williams?" she asked, looking over her thin-framed glasses between my friend and the ream of papers that she was carrying.

"Yes, that's me," Michelle replied, dutifully as ever. *My best friend.*

"I'm Miss Forau, I'm a support counsellor working with the school regarding the recent death of an ex-pupil in the locality."

Michelle, none the wiser, simply nodded, seemingly unequivocally.

"Your head teacher has allowed me to set up a programme

here for students who knew the deceased and are concerned about all the attention and police presence, and to see that every opportunity for support is offered to those who require it."

Michelle invited the young-looking, attractive brunette to sit at her table, yet she still possessed that vacant, lost look in her eyes. She was still racked with emotional turmoil and if I knew it, Amy knew it, too.

"Are you considering speaking to someone about any issues you may be experiencing, Miss Williams?"

Amy—we'll refer to her, humour her, as *Miss Forau*—laid her papers down on the table in front of Michelle's lunch, awaiting an answer.

"No, I don't think so, Miss...?"

"Forau," the fake counsellor finished for her. "My parents are Canadian, but I grew up in Australia."

Michelle smiled at the demon, so taken in by her feminine charm as I once was.

"Nothing like a 'Dildo' *down under!*" the counsellor joked.

Michelle didn't respond, despite the sex-joke being at the bottom of the list of the most unacceptable things to say in this situation—in her bogus position. Perhaps Michelle was too zoned out with her own private thoughts to notice what was said.

"Have the police found anyone yet?" Michelle asked.

Miss Forau flicked through some of the pages in the pile.

"They're slow and shoddy, your police; but, somebody's bound to know something. I have no news here, I'm afraid. But, they're everywhere: in the streets, the shops, in the school. They've assured the public there's nothing to worry about."

Michelle reached into her lunchbox and took out a carton of orange juice. Miss Forau watched her patiently whilst the schoolgirl sucked the drink out through the clear straw.

"Miss Williams, I'm actually concerned about another girl; someone you may know, I believe."

"Who might that be, Miss?"

The counsellor again flicked through her papers, pretending to find the one marked with the answer she sought. "Ah, here we are: Bethany Childs. Do you know her?"

Without hesitation, Michelle told her that she did.

"She's not been at school much this week. Is she okay? Are you her friend at all? Do you know if she had a connection to the boy that was killed?"

I sensed Michelle becoming antsy at the woman's persistence.

"I... don't know, Miss," Michelle told her. "I was supposed to see her last night—at her home, but she had gone out. I waited, but she didn't return by the time I had to leave."

"Hmm, I see," Miss Forau said. "How long have you two been friends, Miss Williams?"

"All of our lives, Miss. We grew up together."

Miss Forau looked up and stared directly into Michelle's eyes. Whether or not she was trying to force some influence on her, it wouldn't have mattered. Being a coveted agent of Hell, she could have stripped the girl naked right there and extracted any bit of information from her and no one would have seen a thing.

"Are you worried about Bethany, Michelle?" tested Miss Forau.

"Why?"

"I've heard some of the other girls talking, and it seems as if she has been through a traumatic experience lately."

The rape, thought Michelle, suddenly. I 'heard' her thinking it. She panicked.

"Her dad died a few years ago, Miss. Maybe that's what it is? I was present at his funeral, and she was devastated by it, but Bethany's strong, Miss—there isn't much that she couldn't pull through."

You're telling me!

Amy's remarkable, sarcastic thoughts now, filtering into my own.

"Yes, you're right, Miss Williams. She sounds like a strong, inspirational young woman—as are you, I suspect. Listen, I'm occupying the room at the end of the music corridor. Anytime you feel you need to talk to someone–about *anything*–then just come knock and see me, okay?"

The pretty counsellor gathered her paperwork, but not before leaning forward and taking hold of Michelle's juice carton. She placed the straw between her lips and sucked.

Michelle, eyes wide in disbelief, could only stifle a laugh. She wasn't angry or offended; in fact, she may have been impressed by this, I'm afraid to admit.

"My goodness!" exclaimed Miss Forau, catching her breath, then putting on that faux innocent-sounding voice. "I haven't sucked that hard since my time at high school!"

She stood up after handing back the empty carton and turned to leave. A few steps on, she heard Michelle calling after her.

"Yes?" she answered back.

"Thanks."

THIRTEEN

"YOU stay away from Michelle; do you hear me?"

Amy, relaxed as ever in the wicker chair, blew out her cheeks, as if tiring of my cautions.

"Did I harm her? Isn't she still alive and well?"

"That's not the point," I said, angrily. I was sitting upon my bed, stroking my cat. It had been left to my mum in recent days, the welfare of the cat.

"Then, what is your point, Bethany?"

"You have no right involving yourself in my relationships! Do what the fuck you want with my attackers, but do not go near my friends or family."

She leaned forward in eagerness, desperate for my answer to the question that lingered irascibly on her tongue:

"Are *you* warning *me*, child?"

"Yes, I am, and I am not a child. Not any longer. I'm sixteen, now."

Amy leaned back and laughed, her waist-bound jewels tinkling like waltzing fairies. I didn't find it funny. Not at all.

"Go on, demon, laugh. It's all been just a big joke to you, hasn't it?"

Amy actually had tears rolling down her cheeks. Who knew demons could cry, even tears in hysterics?

"Oh, Bethany! My sweet Bethany! You're comical when you're mad, do you know that?"

I brushed off her retort and continued to pet my cat, who surely could see the hellish abomination that sat before us, but unlike myself, somehow did not appear to care or become bothered by it.

"I know what you did this morning," she said to me, as if it was casual news. "I can't say if I prefer the bland method of disposal, but that creep had it coming. You know what he was like, right?"

"Yes, but it's not up to me to decide anyone's fate, is it? That's why we have the law, and justice, to appoint the correct punishments."

"Innocent 'til proven guilty? Spare me the moral code, Bethany. Some of them just have it coming. But, you're right; maybe I did overstep the mark with Michelle. You must recognise that I was only stepping in, in your best interests?"

Like a true snake, she was trying to wriggle out of this as cleanly and clear as only she could.

"Well, I'd appreciate it if you would stop."

Amy fell silent. Contemplating, no doubt.

"Then, if you can stop deviating from our line of business—at least until we're done—you'll no doubt be aware of what's next, won't you? The stakes are higher now, Bethany; we have a job to finish."

"An agenda to fill?"

Amy narrowed her eyes.

"The things that must be done? Of course I do. To whom elsewhere have you been speaking, Bethany?"

I shivered. Despite her alluring features and powerful presence, Amy still had the ability to make me scared of her.

"No one. Why?"

Her eyes widened.

"No night-time visitations interrupting your sleep, per chance?"

"Nothing at all. Nothing that you couldn't already know about. You *are* important and powerful enough to be included in the Devil's company, after all."

This attempt at kissing up to her only seemed more patronising, as the silent moments that passed by served only to start peeling back my faux idolisation of her.

Eventually, she withdrew her minor interrogation and stood up.

"We must get ready to go. It's getting dark."

"Where to now?" I asked, wearily, for I had no desire to be overcome by the demonic spirit that squatted within me.

"Have you heard of the tale about the Carpenter who was saved by a porcine herd whilst he travelled east of the Jordan River?"

"No, I don't think so, but I could–"

"There'll be no need, Bethany. I'll tell it to you now since *I* was there. It's in relation to where I'll be taking you tonight. Now, close your eyes, relax, and imagine this wandering artisan…"

*****

Jesus watched as the fettered man staggered towards him from the tomb. With such unnatural strength, the visibly-troubled, tortured man broke free from his bondage and wasted no time in approaching the Carpenter, with fearless eyes and spit watering his mouth, which had turned crookedly into a devilish sneer. Jesus' power had the intensity and ability to precede him, but, in this case, he withheld it and beckoned the unwise man closer. Jesus thought that there may have been a second man present, or that it was maybe a shadow of some unearthly being, watching.

"Come," Jesus said to the man, whom Jesus recognised as being possessed by evil spirits.

The possessed man, now shaking and trembling as he neared the carpenter—whose power now began to emanate from his being and who revealed to the demons living inside of the possessed man that he was indeed, of divine disposition—stopped at once and began to cry and plead for help and aid.

It just so happened that this self-proclaimed 'Son of God' was carrying such priceless remedies. But, as the man stood, his body convulsed, and more saliva erupted from his gob. It was then that his uninvited, internal guests inherent within him managed to speak to the travelling carpenter, in a language no mortal human could understand.

("For you, Bethany, I will translate it here:")

"You say that you are the Son of God, but we know He has no children! Punish us, and we shall see to it that this human suffers a thousand times' over!"

The deep voice was more than one spirit entity; in fact, there may have been a legion of them, all twisting their tangled tongues, fighting to be heard, and they claimed everything belonged to them.

Just as Jesus was about to verbally react, a herd of feeding pigs wandered close by and caught his attention. They were sent to save him from the numerous black angels he had accosted.

"Spirits, you have no business with this man! What can be done so that you will leave his soul alone?"

Like a puppet dangling on frenzied, invisible strings, the man shuddered violently again, a sign to Jesus that he—or rather, the spirits inside of him—were considering their reply carefully.

"We now have knowledge that you are indeed connected to a divine source, on a secret—albeit meaningless—mission to save these imposters from themselves. It's a mistake to think one man can shoulder the sins of humanity on bones alone, for they are made to break under any burden, no matter the integrity of its foundation."

Jesus regarded the man, then the porcine herd which remained in the vicinity.

"Perhaps dark-driven, monstrous entities like yourselves would be better suited to the swine accompanying us here on this day?"

Jesus nodded in the direction of the pig herd, and the possessed man observed them also, as they fed and snorted and grunted.

"Or, perhaps we would enjoy the company of this man, more? He has decadent flesh forged and fired in the kiln of our Lord. We like it here. It's warmer. Tastier."

Jesus raised an eyebrow as a malevolent laughter burst out from inside the man.

"Surely you don't mean 'God'?"

"SATAN!" the legion of voices growled at once, trembling the ground and echoing gutturally throughout the hilly, Gentile region. Rocks that had lay for decades loosened and began rolling down their mountain-faces like stone tears; the sea of Galilee oscillated, despite being previously rid of its storm, shaken by the fearful bellow of the Devil's name.

Jesus didn't flinch nor fret. He particularly did not fear the voices, or the man, or even for the blasphemy that the legion of verbal damnation had committed, but that didn't mean he wanted to stay and discover what they had planned for him.

"I think I'll condemn you to the filthy pigs," Jesus said, "for in them, *you will feel at home."*

He commanded the spirits leave the human at once and enter the starved bodies of the swine. The man shook again, then dropped like a stone to the floor, whimpering like a child in pain. The herd squealed and grunted wildly as the unnatural spirits possessed its numbers, before running them off a nearby cliff and into the cold, unforgiving water below. Despite their forced extraction, the voices rebuked their adversary's power over them as they spilled over the cliff edge, threatening retaliation at Golgotha.

The coming of the pigs had saved this Jew, Jesus of Nazareth; this self-proclaimed 'Son of God.'

But, when the crowd of villagers—who had been frightfully watching the drama unfold before them—came to him, they offered no gratitude or solace. Instead, they begged the carpenter to leave their region at once, and to never return with or without his sorcery.

This 'king' of the Jews, Jesus of Nazareth.

Son.

Of.

God.

FOURTEEN

I could hear the waves in the sea thrashing around like a great party was in full swing on the ocean bed; Amy's ability to tell a tantalising story was, I had long since established, unparalleled, and I truly believe that she had been involved in that ancient Gospel tale in some shape or form.

She hated saying Jesus' name, screwing up her face in disgust every time she mentioned him in order to retell her past. However, I noticed that she didn't care as much when she spoke his Father's name; it sounded like each of these demons' misery and torment and vengeance came from the seed of a notion of a father who chooses to prefer some of his children to the others. In this case, Jesus was the preferred child, and the original angels merely prototypes of an obeying order of disciples that didn't seem too keen on being replaced. I concluded that Amy contended with a serious multitude of 'daddy issues'.

She revelled in twisting the specifics of this bible story, making it seem like Jesus had been in danger the whole time, when I 'knew' that it had been an indication of his supreme power over the spirits and devils that infested the land he walked upon. I think that, after Jesus was successful in the Judaean desert again Satan, they had the audacity to feel they could still win him over to their side. Satan *could* tempt, but could he deliver? Only the Messiah knew the answer to that, and he didn't falter in any one of Satan's tri-attempts. "What are you thinking, Bethany?"

I broke out of my sublime trance. I no longer heard the crashing of the Galilean waves against the rocks, but Amy's probing words rocking in instead.

"Don't you know?"

"I don't wish to be invasive, despite what you think of me. Your thoughts can be your own."

"When it suits you," I said, disparagingly.

"Fuck, Bethany! You talk the talk but when it comes down to it, you buckle and wilfully bend at the knees!"

"What does *that* mean? That I asked to be raped? I invited it?!"

Amy turned away from me, as if she had said too much.

"No, you *look* at me, Amy! Did I ask for any of this?"

"We've been through this–don't waste your breath."

"Wasn't this always going to happen? The assault, you and me–"

"Just as it was written," Amy said, almost pleasingly, thus ending our conversation.

Oh, how I wished to hear those waves again!

*****

A fucking abattoir.

This was the place we ended up (still in the locality), and as soon as the smell hit me, I pieced together the connection between the Gospel tale of Jesus and the demon-man with our location. Swine!

The building appeared around us as we materialised our way illicitly onto its office premises. There were a vast number of unlawful scandals present in places such as this; I could feel the reminiscences of the past slaughtering like a heavy, unforgiving layer. And, of course, the very *real*, very distinctive smell of warm blood…

Bloody sanitation. That's perhaps the most oxymoronic term I could think of for a place like this. Oh, maybe 'humane slaughtering', too–that's another good one. For instance, the building was one-part slaughterhouse, one-part office. Not that the slaughterman would ever be arriving at five in the morning wearing his best three-piece suit; the 'office' side was ridiculously hygienic and sanitised where it should have been, and any or all blood from that day's work had been obsessively washed away in the production side. The killing process ran on manufactured conveyer belts. Hungry ones that seemed to funnel the animals into the areas where the culling occurred.

I could see from where Amy and I were standing, the placement of the production and culling machinery and tools used in the slaughtering process. In the innards of the building, the echoes of pigs still squealed; sheep and lambs still bleated as if a frightened Clarice Starling was around to hear; and the fear from cows that ran from the pneumatic captive bolt or, utilising more contemporary methods–electrocution by using carefully placed electrodes.

I could see far enough into the future, and the FSA would soon be having a ball in here. Undercover exposés would plaster front page tabloids and would go on to become some of the most talked about documentaries on recent British television, despite it being a cruel, Europe-wide problem. The vegans would soon have their day!

Amy was inspecting the stunning pens while I tried to ward off the horrific images that bombarded me with unwanted, unabridged knowledge of the premises.

"Why are we here?" I eventually managed to ask. I didn't feel sick or nauseas, just a bit nervous, for it felt like we were out in the open, able to be caught.

"There's a great deal going on in Hell, Bethany," Amy began, surveying the empty pens and restraining boxes, though, her mind was clearly elsewhere. "There's a commotion at present and it's about to reach its boiling point. You are the cause. Can't you feel it? Doesn't a place like this bring you home?"

"What? The smell? It's like a carnal butcher's shop!"

"It's an abattoir, Bethany," Amy sighed, making fun of me. "You won't find pink balloons and pussycats in here!"

My home. My cat.

"But, why here? Amy, are we alone?"

"You were always alone, Bethany. Until I came to save you!"

She disappeared into thin air, leaving me to my own

troubled thoughts and feelings.

"Cue the sanctimonious shit, again!" I said into the air and silence that was now prevalent around me, but I was really directing my anger at Amy.

He's here: the third one. Find him. Kill him!

I heard Amy's voice as clear as day invading my mind, and as she had the power to hypnotise or control me any way—any time—she wanted, I fell once again under her dreadful spell, and that killer within me, Bethany Chiller, resurfaced with a maddened hunger and ravenous desire for revenge.

FIFTEEN

THE meat that had been hung on the hooks was out to mature, which is what gave it its great-tasting quality. It seemed like an outdated practise overall, considering the vacuum-packed, wet-aged beef that had been processed here and in other, more modern, plants. Still, it was all about the consumer in the end; they get what they pay for.

The cold, iron-infused smell of blood and meat met with the demonic girl's sense of smell as she entered the earthly realm through her bodily portal; her nose lifted at the metallic-like odour, seeking out the source (though, it was everywhere). Her black hair ponytailed on its own as a strong gust of wind tore through the area where she stood. Then, she suddenly lifted off the ground, appearing to hover, before flying to the source of the wind.

A young man in overalls and carrying a toolkit, entered stage left of this slaughter-theatre, from where the side door to the building was situated (and the source of the draught). He wasn't on the roster for this evening but engaging in some overtime to help fix the machinery that operated non-stop and full-force during the day.

The girl in the air, Bethany Chiller, had eyes that were as black and flammable as coal, but which could see as clearly as any microscope could the pores on your skin, spied him from over fifty yards away as he entered.

She glided downward out of his view as he crossed the plant floor to a steel, cylinder-shaped machine that was a pig scalder and dehairer: a machine that tersely rotated each individual hog after being submerged in hot water, to remove it of its hair, hence its name. This rough circular shaver of sorts rattled the creature 'round 360° while shedding its oils and fats and other bits of carcass into specialised equipment. Externally, it looked like a bulky portable barbecue.

This was the machine that Wayne was carrying the tools for. Had she not known him for the disgusting deed he had carried out, she may never *have thought this bright, young man capable.*

He got to the machine a minute or so later; by this time, Bethany had moved closer to it–to him–and was preparing her attack. She watched him through the blood-dyed, plastic sheet–the bit that caught the excess parts of the pig that flew out as it revolved–as he worked on greasing the drive chain and bearings, tightening nuts here and there among a lingering smell of swine, blood and metal.

It only took him twenty or so minutes to accomplish the task, but to Bethany, spying on him with demonic, murderous intent, it felt like forever. Flames flashed intermittently from her bare palms, eager to ignite, to scorch flesh…

Wayne–one-third responsible for holding Bethany down and was, in order of each one's demise, her third attacker/victim–felt like someone was watching him; though, he was certain he was the only employee on the site at this hour. He began to feel spooked, uneasy; so much death occurred here, and it was grim in the silence.

There was a beeping sound that repeated from the panel interface, and water suddenly began pouring into the machine. Wayne noticed that the water discharge caps hadn't been removed, as well as the hose which fed the water in, and by now the double rollers were half-submerged. Red lights activated on the interface let him know that the heating elements were operating at near-full capacity. All this, while he had a stunned expression on his face.

Wayne quickly turned away from the hot machine, but he got caught by a spray of scalding water. He had only been sent to carry out maintenance work on the pig dehairer, not play with it. He couldn't work out how it had started in automatic mode. He hadn't hit any of the interface's buttons…

As the lid began to shudder before it was due to begin closing over, Wayne found himself stuck to the edge of the machine. He wasn't caught on anything, no clothing snagged or tucked inside any crack or crevice; he found that he just couldn't hop off the damn thing.

And then the girl walked into view.

She was a wild sight; not an inch of her said 'Good Samaritan' to him, but from where did he recognise that pretty face and black hair? The rising steam from the water obscured his vision of her as she walked through it and closer to him.

"Help!" Wayne cried, feeling his skin wetting. "I'm stuck, and the machine is on auto-start!"

Bethany now stood mere inches from him.

I know who you are! Wayne thought to himself, and at this point the incident at the Halloween party returned.

"I know you!" he then said to her, as if this admission would save him.

The girl lunged forward and grabbed his overalls by the collar, pulling him to her, yet he remained seated.

"You have no idea who I am!" she screamed, above the boiling water and spinning rollers.

She pushed him backward; he cut the back of his head on the lid as it completed its crescent path—on its program to begin the process of dehairing and scalding the enclosed subject.

He screamed his last words to her as the unrelenting rollers spun him under the scalding pool of water. The boiling water stripped off his skin almost immediately after the rollers made light work of his overalls. Before the lid on his metal coffin closed entirely, he glimpsed the girl through the sweltering steam, and her eyes were as black as coal.

It looked almost as if there was a camel beside her.

Lord, how long wilt thou look on?
Rescue my soul from their destructions,
my darling from the lions.

Psalms 35:17

"HELL IS ON ITS WAY"
5th NOVEMBER

ONE

LIFE is one of the most complicated things we'll ever go through. In fact, it's really *everything* most of us will ever experience. It's the sharpest double-edged sword, being both meaning*ful* and meaning*less* in not-so-equal measures. Sure, it's one of the shortest travels we're apt to blister our feet on, but it's by no means easy or sympathetic. Take it from me. What I've seen, what I know, *what I've done*, has been like the door for which my power has the key to unlock: so many mysteries, so many unanswered questions.

That's not what this power is for. Doing Hell's homework like some bullied child is what I've become, with Amy as my intimidator. I'm cleaning up mess on Earth that I feel God should be more hands-on with. Like, where is His brush and pan? Why am I on my hands and knees, covered in blood–the blood of *my* victims–whilst His Almighty ass sits on a throne of gold or whatever. It's not fair. Which is another thing…

Life isn't fair. All men are equal, and all that! What about us women!? Are we not equal too? Surely my current status contradicts everything? Sorry, I feel like I'm dragging you into some infernal feminist movement. That's not what these pages are for and is not nowhere near to the crushing finale that's much closer.

Bonfire Night. As apt as any evening for bringing forth the flames of Hell–which is exactly what I did. My decisions up until that point were solely in conjunction with my twisted doppelganger, the ferocious demon counterpart, Bethany Chiller; and I feared that for my last victim she would resurface indefinitely, leaving me to become entrapped in my own body like a pseudo comatose patient. Her power certainly

144

felt strong enough. But I had to resist being overthrown. The problem was, I was losing my strength. With each minute, each *kill*, I was ebbing away from the girl I once was; my identity was being pushed into the shadows—no, *pulled*—and I knew it would be only a matter of time before 'Miss Childs' was lost forever.

What I needed to do was not only resist Amy, but to confront her, too, and do whatever it took to defy Hell's takeover of my once-innocent soul.

Only then could I ask His forgiveness.

*****

The local area swarmed with police. The abattoir was closed for the day; it was a funny sight, seeing lorryloads of pigs and sheep being herded into transport to be culled at another facility. It was last-minute, small-scale panic, like the foot-and-mouth debacle after the first anniversary of the turn of the century—just without the quarantine and vaccination of the livestock.

That aside, there wasn't much else the authorities could be doing. This death appeared to be a tragic accident, unlike Mike's death (which they had deemed as suspicious, despite unearthing nothing that would support murder) or Shaun, who remained missing. With any luck, these beasts were serving their sentences in Hell. And Graeme? I don't think anyone cared about him. They scooped him up off the road like you would ice-cream out of the tub.

I found myself back in bed. My whole existence shrouded in darkness, blanketed by my duvet. It was just before 1 P.M. I was certain it was the weekend.

The building of the bonfire, an annual ritual among the locals, had seen their wooden offering top well over twenty-feet in the weeks since its conception. Someone would be tasked to douse it in flammable liquid, before it would go on to light up the area for a few hours as the community, rocked and puzzled as they were in recent days, would come together for the event and enjoy the artificial lightshow of flame and fireworks.

This was no longer my scene. I couldn't mix with people anymore. I had also developed a hatred of such jovial activities. I felt more inclined to be fed by the darkness and succumb to its hospitality, as opposed to going back to mixing with society. Maybe Amy's agenda was winning? It seemed near-impossible then, that I could break free from her, such was her hold on me.

I had to speak to Michelle again. I didn't plan on frightening her but at this point I had to do something to get someone else on my side, despite what I had become; someone neutral who would understand and hopefully not freak out. Yes, Michelle would be that person.

I sensed she was at home too, in her room. Like my own, her thoughts were hazy, a mixed-up jumble of emotions and opinions that were all reluctant to be at ease. She was in mental pain; our sudden break this week, my attack, everything was piling on top of her. I had to see her again and put some answers in her mind to pacify the questions that rattled around in there.

I had to do it. The ultimate way of showing Michelle what I had become: I willed myself from my room to hers. It only took a moment's thought, a second that meant nothing to the universe or Heaven and Hell; a rip in some cosmically-divine fabric that meant an entity moving in spaces that no other physical body could.

TWO

"NO, that's not what I'm seeing!"

"It's okay, Michelle," I said, after fully appearing by her wardrobe. I had been conscious of how I looked, so I presented myself in my jeans and hooded top, and my hair, wild as ever. But, zero makeup. Even the *Chiller* bitch within didn't stir.

"Bethany... how did... tell me what the fuck's going on?"

"That's why I'm here, to speak to you."

"What you just did... Coming out of the air like that! Bethany, what happened to you?"

I sat on her double bed and beckoned her beside me. I couldn't believe how understanding she was being, despite what had happened. I think that when she saw it was me materialising out of the empty air in her room, her fear left her, flying away like a startled bird.

"Something *did* happen to me, Michelle, and it was nobody's fault except..."

"Tell me, Bethany! We're in this together!"

"Only *you're* not, Michelle! And I'd like to try keep it that way. Please–for your own safety. For your life."

She regarded me dolefully, but I was not one to be pitied. I took her hand in mine. She was trembling, lightly. Her anxiety weighted me.

"It happened that night I was raped," I began unfolding, "when I got home. Someone was waiting for me there."

"Your mum? You've told her everything by now, right?"

"No, Michelle," I said, "there's absolutely no way she could ever find out about it, or what came next."

Michelle appeared to have accepted my irresponsibility and

disregard for my own being. Humility and self-sacrifice have my name plastered all over them, it seems.

"There was a woman in my room," I said, understanding myself the Sapphic implication of that night-time visitation, "and she claimed to know me. Said she had known me for a long time; she even knew about things that happened to me when I was younger."

"Did she know your mum?"

"No," I said. "Just me."

Michelle leaned forward and hugged me. I could feel her sobbing.

"We need to get you help, Bethany. A doctor or counsellor– just anyone who can help fix this whole fucking mess!"

"I am fixing it, Michelle."

I think it was at that moment the penny dropped. She started thinking about the young guy killed in the restaurant and from the social media leftovers she had picked up regarding the abattoir incident.

"Were those the ones who hurt you?"

My own eyes, brimming with tears: "Yes, they were."

"And you've hurt them back?"

Michelle spoke slowly, piecing it all together in her mind.

"They're dead, Michelle! It's all Amy's doing!"

"Amy? Is that the woman from your room?"

I nodded, obediently, as Michelle handed me a tissue from the box on her bedside cabinet. I wiped away the tears and blew my nose into the Kleenex.

"How is it all her doing?"

I couldn't really put into words a description of the power I possessed, so I decided to just show her. Careful not to harm her, I began, literally, playing with fire: smokeless orbs, orange, spherical fireballs, that flew from my hands and around the room; rainbow-arched flames flew one palm to the other; and the fire in my eyes lit up the room even brighter than the afternoon light from outside.

Michelle's eyes darted left and right, up and down, as she studied and feared the floating fire-orbs; she gasped as waves of searing hot flames bounced between my palms, disappearing into each metacarpal space without causing any damage or inflicting pain.

"Bethany... is this some kind of magic?"

"The Devil's," I said, and clasped my hands together. The orbs extinguished in mid-air and the hot air abated.

We sat in silence for a minute or so, to let each of us take in what had been displayed. I felt more ashamed that I had to resort to doing what I did there to get her to believe me. I was stripping her of *her* choice of what to have a belief in.

Then, finally, Michelle spoke first.

"I don't get this—*real* magic, or the David Blaine stuff?!"

"It's as real as you or me," I revealed. "A gift from Hell, courtesy of Amy."

"Like, *actual* Hell?"

"The very place," I remarked, but not boastfully.

"But, how can this be?" Michelle began to get flustered. "What gift? Who is this Amy, really? Hell?"

"I didn't believe in any of it at the start, either," I started to explain. "But then Amy told me things, *showed* me things, that proved it all. She said she was sent to see I got justice for what they did to me."

"And you're their jury *and* executioner now?"

"Bestowed upon me, it seems," I sighed. "You see, Amy initiated me into what she called her 'infernal cabal'. She is witness to the revenge killings, Michelle. So, they pay for what they did to me. On one hand, she's avenging my broken body; on the other, I'm afraid because it's doing something to me internally, Michelle. She demonised me and my name. I am now her creation: Bethany Chiller is my other self."

"There's two of you?"

"Not quite; we inhabit the same body: mine. She is the source of my power. I am the reason she is here."

"Bethany, I'm having a tough time getting 'round all of this. As far out there as it seems, I believe you. So, Amy is like, what? A guardian angel, or something?"

"Far from it! Demonic to the core, she is, judging from her

background and the tales she's told. It's like, when you speak to her, you're talking with someone who's manipulated plenty of the world's elite; partied with the monstrous of them all and drunk them under the table."

"Do you believe everything she's told you?"

"I have no reason to doubt her, Michelle."

"Where is she now?"

"I don't know where she goes in her downtime," I truthfully told, "but I do know that she's always watching, listening, probably even now. Hi, Amy!"

"Hey! Don't push her. She might come knocking!"

I laughed. Somehow, I laughed.

"Well, what's your next step?"

"My dad told me to hold on, try to resist until the end," I said, aware that this titbit of information could be picked up by Amy's ever-listening ears, but I didn't care. I could feel things coming to an end and if there was going to be a confrontation of sorts, best to let it happen.

"He's in Hell, too?"

"No! But he visits me in my dreams and in that short while, I feel like none of this is even happening. It's just a nightmare—mine. You know, if only I could've saved him, Michelle. With this power now, I *could* have saved him."

"Bethany, honey, I hate to ask but judging by the sound of things, who's going to save you?"

We softly, playfully, bumped our heads together just then—yin and yang, remember?—and sobbed.

THREE

AMY had heard everything that Michelle and I poured our hearts out over. Yes, she had once said something about how my personal life was not completely in her interests, but we both know that's bullshit, right? Her ears began burning the second I entered Michelle's room, and not a minute sooner.

I decided to walk back home. Again, I was followed by invisible *things*; things with hawkish whispering, their intents and purposes not all lost on a sixteen-year old girl. I ignored them the best I could, but my heart still thudded with fear.

Everything was falling apart for me; for Amy, it was all falling into place. Whatever deal she had pitched to the monarchs of Hell surely had them rubbing their hands at this point, as with each kill that took place my soul was indeterminately becoming their 'property'. And by that, I don't mean in their possession: it meant having me overtaken by this monstrous being inside me that I helped to create, and thus, another loss for the kingdom of Heaven. A victory for the forces of darkness, and a crushing defeat for the Almighty–if I should say so myself.

I had to remain strong, didn't I? Hadn't my father hinted at some sort of recompense if I could resist Amy's plan 'til it was all over? And when would that be, exactly? Tonight? Tomorrow? Decades from now?

It's getting late now. The sun will be up in a couple of hours. If I haven't lost you this far, then stay with me until the very end, please. Until first light, at least.

Any light.

FOUR

AMY greeted me with all the charm and affection of one who lusts after her desires and who usually succeeds in getting what they want. Cavorting in my room with me after I returned home, the smile on her face seemed as if it could never be removed, even with holy water.

"I'm happy for you," she said.

"Why? What for?"

She looked around, mockingly, as if there were others in hiding trying to listen in.

"For telling your friend about us!"

"I didn't tell her about *us*, Amy. There is no *us*, whatever you think the hell that is."

I was mad at her for eavesdropping. I knew she would.

"Oh, on the contrary, my sweet," she said, sprinkling that sweetness into her language as if I was craving a sugary rush from her, "you and I are going to be the best of friends very soon. Maybe even more, if you'd like? We'll make such a pair!"

I regarded her angrily.

"Look, just because you had your talons inside me at the beginning of all of this does not mean I want to pursue any kind of relationship with…"

"Go on: with…?"

"A bitch from Hell!" I said to her face, direct and full of teen gusto.

"My! You've certainly been stoking the fires of confidence lately, Bethany! I can't figure out what your problem is, but if you maybe spoke to me, I would be able–"

"I don't *want* to speak to you, Amy! There's nothing but pain and horror every minute you take me out there! Haven't

152

we done enough? Haven't I killed enough to be damned forever?"

I threw myself down on the bed, crying. I felt Amy lying down beside me, her arm slithering over my thinning frame, until she rested her hand under my chest. In a few moments, she was spooning me. I also felt the trinket that was tied at her midriff pressing against the small of my back.

"Don't be like that, Bethany," she spoke softly, consoling me. "I didn't mean to hurt you."

I didn't feel like speaking to her, so I let her have her way with her vibrant libretti.

"Let me tell you something about what it used to be like. In the beginning, it was beautiful! Bethany, we had everything we could ever want: all the love and prayers your heart could hold. Never wanting for anything–never *needing* anything, to be exact. And, hey, I loved my Father then, too. Very much. *Too* much, it seemed. But, being obedient to one's parent brought with it its own heartache–that I was missing out on a mother's love. God has so much love to give, Bethany, but it's infrequent and reserved for a select few. He'll never tell you that, but it's there for all to see.

"Then one day, we were called–gathered, I should say–at the feet of another; one who also promised us the same things our Creator had, and yet more. I became besotted by his rising power, his bold determination, but his hostility toward our siblings and our Father unnerved us. That's when the first war for Heaven began.

"It's easy to point the finger of blame when you're the Almighty, isn't it? Course it is. We would have won that battle if only our great leader, Lucifer, had shown some sensibility in his attack. Rousing only a third of our brethren, we knew that any amount less than half would be hopeless, but we charged on regardless. Bethany, blood filled the clouds! And when it rained, it rained red on the lands below. Can you imagine what that was like? We were rebels as we were slung into the abyss; God's shadow–that's what the abyss is, you know? Because He chooses not to turn around and acknowledge us that are in it—what we once were… His mistakes… His *children*… I miss my Father, too.

"Bethany, are you still awake…?"

I vaguely registered Amy removing her hand from under me; as she suspected, I was indeed nodding off. I hadn't taken in much of what she had said, but I believed it all. Then, in that mixed state of being asleep and awake, I could feel the mattress of the bed rising slightly as her body vanished into the air to leave me alone, and for her to sit in the loneliness of her own company of hurt.

FIVE

THE crowds that had gathered in the pitch-black evening filled most of the grass space around the leisure centre, close to an old war memorial and library. It was a privately-funded event, and one that was sponsored by local businesses who had supplied most of the fireworks and snack bars for the evening. All that was required from the community was the large amount of wood, furniture and the like, to be set ablaze.

I awoke from my slumber, sans visit from my father. Oh, how I needed him then! He likely would have supplied me with words to help me get through the rest of the night.

I was groggy, irritated; yet, at the same time, I was marvelling inside, possibly due to this Bethany Chiller identity stirring, as she prepared to surface again. I had an agitated feeling that tonight was the night it would all come to a head.

My mum knocked on my bedroom door, before slowly opening it and poking her head in.

"Bethany? You awake?"

Though I was lying down facing away from the door, I didn't have the heart to fake it. It was not fair on either of us.

"Yeah, mum, I'm awake," I replied.

She stepped in, quietly still, as if she still thought I was ill. I suppose I was and had been exhibiting the effects of a seasonal flu or long-term womanly pains for the last few days.

"Can I speak to you?"

"Of course." I rolled 'round to face her entirely.

She sat considerately at the end of the bed, beside where the cat was lying in a circle position and shape not unlike the Greek ouroboros. Her tail wasn't being fed to her, though.

155

"How have you been?" she asked me, without the slightest sign of insincerity.

"I'm good," I lied.

She regarded me with eyes that knew me better than I knew myself; was sending worrisome thoughts telepathically that were concerned about my current condition.

"You're not looking that good, sweetheart, and I haven't seen much of you this week. Haven't even had a minute to give you your birthday gifts!"

I smiled reassuringly. There was nothing wrong that she had done or anything that she didn't do—except gave birth to me all those years ago.

"I'm *fine!*" I reiterated, emphasising the word.

"And school?"

"Just gearing up for the Christmas rush, now that we've got Halloween out of the way."

Halloween. My nightmare.

"Okay," my mum sighed. "It's just that we seem to have been off this week. I dunno… Maybe I should reconsider the extra hours over the festive holiday? I don't want you here in the house alone if you're unwell."

I sat up; step by step, it seemed, for my mum had to lean forward and grab me to pull me. But it was an achievement on my part, showing her that I was capable of managing. Or, at least, initiating.

"No, don't do that," I urged, settling the covers to hide my bottom half. I was still bruised around *that* area and I didn't want anything introducing itself. "You'll miss out on a great payday! Which means *I'll* miss out, too!"

Again, her eyes (eyes that once set upon my father and fell in love with him; love strong enough to marry and bear his child and retain the memory of him in her heart for years to come) set upon me, looking for any deceit, any kind of falseness on my part, which would have been noticeable if she'd only been imbued with the power and knowledge I had.

Against my wishes, I had to fake everything. That I was alright, that I hadn't suffered a fall-out with Michelle, and that

I'd go to see the doctor about the crippling period pains I was experiencing.

Before she left, my mum stopped at the door and said, "You know, Bethany, that's *some* look for you!"

"What look, mum?"

"The crazy hair and make-up that you're rocking. I don't know what the hell you were thinking!"

SIX

AMY had secured the boy tightly to the pole–his wooden stake–with thick cord. She had also knocked out some of his teeth, for the blood ran out of the gag his gums chomped on and down his neck and exposed upper body. For some reason she had completed the task by hand. Perhaps she enjoyed the physical thrill of the fight with the pitiful human she viewed as garbage.

"Stay still and I'll see to it that you live just a little bit longer!" Amy threatened him. His terrified eyes never left her; both tear- and blood-stained as they were.

He tried to mumble something, but the unusually strong woman with claws for fingernails and glowing, red orbs for eyes, pressed a threatening finger to his lips.

"And don't try to make a sound, either! You'll burn alive a thousand times' over if you do!"

The young man refrained from resisting further. His face, crookedly lined with sweat and blood that ran from his scalp (where she had pulled him by his hair from his employer's vehicle, out the driver's window during his lunch break); ached worse than he'd ever experienced before. The woman grabbed his head and positioned it so he could only look forward, then tightened a thick rope around his neck that looped around the stake he was tethered to.

"Consider this your auto-da-fé! There's someone familiar that you're going to meet soon, and with your help, she'll be mine forever! Thank you for doing what you four did to her..."

He had no idea who this woman was or why she had brought him here (or even what she had against him), where weak rays of a dying sun's light broke in through unequal slits and crevices, into this dry, enclosed, wood-piled sarcophagus.

His tomb.

His final resting place.
This pre-lit bonfire.

SEVEN

WITHOUT linking with Amy, I knew exactly what I had to do and where I had to go.

I showered and re-dressed into something that was a blast from earlier that week: my zombie cheerleader outfit. Not the original, of course (I still don't know where the hell that disappeared to) but one that I was able to 'magic up' and fit back into. Everything bar the pom-poms, at least. I didn't see the need for those.

I don't know why, but something told me that I had to dress this way; that things were coming full circle and I needed to emulate the look and style I wore on that fateful Halloween night.

I pigtailed my hair, slapped on the appropriate make-up, and I swear if you were to have seen me that evening, you'd have thought you had stepped back in time to the Monday before, when I first sported this look. It was uncanny.

Before my door mirror, where only a handful of days ago I tried to imitate Samantha Baker, I stared at myself–at the *reproduction* of who I once was. The world would never again be the way I remembered; that much I had allowed myself to give in to. There was no use fighting it–college would be a no-no; finishing high school would certainly be out of the question. I had my earlier grades on paper at home–what use were they now?

I just had to get this night over with. Eternity could wait.

#####

The crowd appeared to be multiplying at every half hour down by the entry into the industrial location, where the locals held their magnificent Bonfire event. I had been to several over the years, with and without my parents. I stopped going after my father passed. By 7 P.M. music was blaring, everyone was cheering, and the structure of well-placed old furniture was doused in petrol, with a looming countdown prepped before it was to be set alight. I was watching from the air, my eyes as black as night so no flames attracted anyone to my presence. I also had to be wary of any rogue fireworks coming my way, so I created an energy field around me, just in case. It was like a bubble around me.

I heard Amy calling to me in my mind.

Bethany…

Where are you?

We're in the bonfire, Bethany…

We?

In the centre—hurry…

EIGHT

IT wasn't hard to miss the poor, disfigured soul tied to his own personal gibbet at the heart of the bonfire. He witnessed me materialising in front of him, and I knew that he recognised me, too. The outfit gave it away, of course, but also, I think he regretted the whole scene.

This was Steven, the one who tore me open first.

We were deep in the mountain of broken furniture and trade palettes and many other combustibles. Amy was standing impatiently by Steven, like the Roman soldier who had speared Jesus' side at Calvary; she had a serpent's tail that rose behind her like it had a mind of its own; her skin was blood-red; and her mouth fanged, desperate to tear into flesh. Every bit as brutal and brandishing.

"I want to speak to him first," I said to Amy.

The noise from the crowd outside of the pyre kept at bay while the three of us somehow managed to roam around undetected in the bowels of the wood pile. I could smell the fuel from the jerrycan that the teenager was using to prepare for ignition.

"We've not got much time, Bethany! They'll be lighting his inferno shortly!"

"Just remove his gag," was all I asked of her.

Amy did as she was told. Steven spat out a blob of thick blood and drew in an enormous breath. Surprisingly, he didn't attempt to shout or look for help. Amy must have really put the frighteners in him to do otherwise.

I stepped closer to him, my pigtails draping down over my shoulders, drawing the focus to the half-heart pendant above my breasts. I knew Steven noticed it. It was the first thing he'd spotted when he had been on top of me.

"You know what you did to me, so I won't go over it again. Because of that night, your friends are dead, and you will join them. But, not by *my* hand."

Amy suddenly dropped her fearsome stance. "Not by *your* hand? Bethany, explain!"

"Whatever punishment you think he needs, you carry it out, demon! I'm going home. I'm done with all of the death; all the misery. It's not who I am."

I turned away from the two of them; I heard Steven try to mash some words from the bloody mess that was his mouth.

"Bethany, is it? I am so s-sorry. I do know who you are. What we did t-to you was unforgiveable, inexcusable."

I turned back to look at the young man, and I truly felt for him. I knew he would be killed and could end up in Hell. Then, Amy slapped him hard, spilling more blood.

"You weak fool! Tell her what you *really* mean to say!"

Steven's head jerked upward as if an invisible hand had forcibly palmed it.

"No, we enjoyed what we did to you, bitch! So sweet and juicy and virginal! You'll never have that back! We own it! We own you!"

I knew Amy was controlling him, skewering this bizarre situation to reach an outcome that satisfied her. He was acting as her puppet—as I had been.

"I will not kill him, Amy!"

"But you're not freeing him, are you? So, you are participating in his demise! Face it, Bethany—this is the culmination of our efforts to avenge you! Finish it and you'll be free forever! Hell is coming for you and you're marked. It knows where you are always!"

I knew exactly what she was hinting at. Finish it… and you'll be MINE forever.

I walked back to Amy, my imitation canvas shoes with the black and red laces stepping upon splintering wood. We were face to face; I could feel the heat flowing from her body, her murderous passion and vehement intent; her tail wavering and on the offensive.

"Listen: it's not going to happen. I may be below Heaven, but I'm above Hell, demon, and I will stand my ground. My will be done,

Gomory!" I whispered, staring her dead in the eyes.

I could tell she wanted to scream abuse and lash out at me, but she could not. Not since I knew her true identity. Demons—all smoke and mirrors! It was blatantly obvious what—who—this fiend truly was. I dare say you've managed to figure it out yourself, haven't you? Early on, I did. 'Amy' just happened to be the fifty-sixth demon Duke, Gomory, a very nasty, very masculine creature who procures the love and attention of distressed young maidens. Someone like… myself? Disguising himself as a lustful, gorgeous woman was evidently more successful than appearing as his true, lurid self.

I suppose Gomory should have seen it coming, too. The charm around his waist; the appearances on the great camel, all signatures of Gomory, (who did congregate with the upper echelons of Hell's dark society) which should have been kept hidden. I've investigated his past and it is a grim study of biblical heft. The incident in the bonfire was merely just the tip of his infernal iceberg.

"You! You don't know me! I made you, Bethany! You're mine!"

I somehow found the strength and tenacity to sport a wicked smile and offer a wink; this enraged the creature even more. It appeared to view me as the traitor, becoming shocked and flustered at the fact I knew who it really was—and what that really meant for me. All the time Steven regarded us left and right.

Amy retreated from me and slunk into a shadowed part of the bonfire's bowels where she remained unseen. At that moment, the bonfire was lit.

NINE

IT was too late to do anything about Steven's predicament, but I honestly did not want to leave him to die this way. With my claws I tried to separate him from the pole that Amy had secured him to, but with transcendent magic she had bound him for good. I could only offer his soul words of comfort if I could not save his body.

"For with the heart one believes and is justified, and with the mouth one confesses and is saved," I said to the frightened young man, who listened upon these words acceptingly and, dare I say, humbly, for he knew his end was near.

Beyond us, the cheering and music roared; the fireworks flew and blasted, and the flames from the exterior of the bonfire began to creep inside to where we stood, hot and tempered by our predicament.

I touched Steven's face, stroked his cheek, and took away his fright and numbed his pain. It was the least I could do.

"Thank you, Bethany," he said to me, breathlessly. "Not a day has went by that I haven't regretted that awful, evil thing we did to you. Forgive me."

Before the flames encroached into the cavity—into his heated chamber—I did what I knew I could only have done, and that was to disappear. I felt bad for it, but all Steven would have experienced of his demise was seeing the flames burn away the malevolence from his being since I'd removed the ability for him to feel any painful sensation.

As I found myself flying aimlessly through the air, invisible to all but the heavens, the bonfire collapsed in on itself in a loud, crushing mess that sent fiery embers metres high into the air. I looked back only once, knowing that his soul had crossed over, but to where I did not care.

TEN

I guess I roamed the night sky for some time, not looking, not searching, for after a time most activity below ceased: lights went out in houses; bonfires all over the land were dying down; and life just seemed to slow down.

Before I went home, I flew by the house where the horror all began. Nothing out of the ordinary there. I felt that I had to be in the proximity of the night where it all changed for me; where and when life took on a different meaning and truths were realised. I stayed only for a few minutes, expelling all the unwanted negative energies that remained. It was then that I realised: I had taken control of Bethany Chiller–she *hadn't* killed tonight! I was conscious of every step I'd made since leaving the house!

With this astounding revelation, I made my way back home.

*****

Amy was sitting in the wicker chair, her face spoilt and angry and disappointed.

"What are you doing here?" I asked. "Gomory?"

"So, you know who I am, do you?"

It was strange, but she seemed close to tears, as if on the brink of some wondrous defeat.

"You left so many obvious clues," I said, beginning to unwind. It was in the early hours of Sunday morning: the Sabbath. "You didn't think I'd fall for this magazine-model charade, did you?"

"Bethany, don't forget that we had a deal." Her tone changed. She seemed to want dialogue, communication, faster and harder–to the point.

"Tell me those terms again, demon," I demanded. "And tell me you didn't try to fuck me over in any of it! More importantly, tell me what you *really* wanted from me: my body? My pain? My *soul?*"

Amy looked me up and down. "I like your outfit. I have the original, still."

"Well, you can keep it because that's all you're ever getting from me. Now, Amy–Gomory–whatever you want to be called, I *command* you to leave me alone from now on now that I know your true name."

"You think you can hurt me just because you know my–"

I walked over and slapped her face as she sat in the chair. It was the hardest open-palmed strike I have ever given anyone in my life.

I had bruised her cheek and eye, maybe even split the skin.

"Get out, Amy! And never come back!"

My anger was intensifying; I still possessed the demonic power that Amy had given me, and it was revealed in the flames in my eyes and the fire burning in my palms.

"Okay, because you said so this time; and only because you're hurting, babe. But I'll come back. Maybe not today or in a week, but we will see each other again. You can count on that."

She stood up in front of me so close our noses nearly touched. I thought she was about to kiss me.

"Are you sure you don't want to change your mind? You can keep the gift, you'll use it again sooner or later."

Her beautiful dark eyes were trying to probe into mine, likely seeking a way into my mind to influence my answer. I think she even tried stroking my hair.

"Above Hell, demon…" I reminded her, gritting my teeth.

"But "below Heaven", right? Hold onto that position, Bethany. You may just be one of His reserved few."

She smiled, looked away; realising she had lost this fight, she slid by me to the mirror upon the back of my door. She stepped through it as if it were a rectangular pane of clear nothingness, but not before twisting her head back 'round to get in the last word:

"Remember, Bethany: it's better to light a candle than curse the darkness," she advised, mockingly, then disappeared into the shimmering frame, and out of sight.

I sat in the wicker chair, exhausted in every way conceivable. I didn't want to cry; I wanted to laugh! Yes, laugh! At the absurdity of it all! Talk about a bad week!

For Amy, I was, and always had been, her instant obsession. Whatever the figures in Hell had planned was to be put on hold for the time being. They couldn't have me now, but I had a feeling they would not let a little thing like 'time' get in the way.

As for my attackers, I don't care nor wish to know where they are in the afterlife. I can still remember what they did to me, thrust after thrust; and although at times I still feel their hands holding me down, I am no longer their prisoner.

EPILOGUE

THAT was *not* a pleasant story. If you were upset by any of it then let me offer you some consolation by saying that, even though it's been about a week since the end of it all, I have accepted it as part of my personal history.

Bethany Chiller still rents my body, and she pays for this by letting me dip into her powers now and again (such as using my eyes as fire to light these pages).

Maybe I should just burn this text. I mean, who'd really want to read it? It's far-fetched, it's delirious, it's god-damn blasphemous! Yet, it's all true, and I know because I lived it.

Amy/Gomory will come back one day, I know it. I can say that they won't be getting an easy time of it in Hell just now. I mean, letting one like myself slip through their fingers like that when they were so close to sealing the deal! They dish out heavy punishments down there, and if I don't see her for many years, it'll be because they will be nursing a very sore backside!

My father hasn't returned, but he saved me, I believe. He helped me resist Amy's agenda–her final kill quota–and I have to thank him and his heavenly light source for that. Thanks, dad; I love you and I know you'll fight my corner to get me in beside you when the time comes.

I suppose I owe you some gratitude too, for being patient and sitting with this lonely sixteen-year old girl while she inscribed her frantic ramblings into her notebook. It's been my therapy, my rock, somewhere I could turn and dump everything that weighed on my mind. Without your presence, I may not have been able to cope with it in the easy-going way I have tonight. And if you have any questions or queries, save 'em 'til we meet in Heaven! I'll be all ears then.

Well, it looks like the first glimpse of the sun is coming up–you stayed until the light, like I asked. For that I am grateful. Eternally.

*****

My period just started…

THE TENT
A Bethany Chiller® memory

ONE

THERE was already damage in Bethany Childs' mind long before the attack ever took place; an area occupied by corruption which, even in her supernatural state, refused to go away. Memories would be recycled until it was time for a reboot that would send the grimmest contents to the very front.

Before her fate exposed itself in the most dreadful and undignified of ways, snippets of her future had been evident throughout her childhood. Watching a late-night horror show; skimming over a TV sex ad; were all puzzles in a jigsaw that had mapped out Bethany's young life. Had she been more aware of the enigmatic clues thrown up at her in her pubescence, Bethany might have heeded their warnings.

But Bethany had her revenge on those who wronged her. Perhaps in the eyes of God and the Devil, their punishment was justified. Merciless, but retributed accordingly. This was no place to recount their horror or their crime.

It had been the tent. It was one of the earliest signs; that ghastly tabernacle sitting undisturbed in the sweeping country fields, which heralded her doom. It is here our story begins.

TWO

THE trip to Aunt Jennifer's had been Bethany's second of that tense summer, the first having been to rescue the woman from her abusive husband, Uncle Mick. Bethany's dad—Aunt Jennifer's older brother—had given him a lesson in bare-knuckle boxing that day that Bethany was sure Uncle Mick would never forget. The young girl had witnessed her father beating the alcoholic with such ferocity that the image of the bloodied, bruised face of Uncle Mick had never left her, even in dreams.

Dad drove quietly with the sun visor down, while her mother sat to his left cradling a basket of home-baked foods: gifts for Aunt Jennifer. Her parents were a happy couple, Bethany noted; an argument rarely came between them. Married as high-school sweethearts with one beautiful child. Other than the family disturbance that was Uncle Mick, life was generally sound to them.

"Are you going to play with Stephen?" mum asked, looking over her shoulder.

Bethany took notice. She had been watching the blue sky above the swaying green and yellow fields. A colourful mix, like something she had painted in her art class.

"Of course," she replied. "We get on well, don't we?"

"I know you do," mum spoke again, "only he's had it a bit rough lately, with his dad being away for a bit and Aunt Jennifer taking unwell. If there's anyone who could cheer that boy up, it's you, Bethie."

Bethie! She despised that abbreviation of her beautiful name. But the woman who had decided to bless her with it retained more right than anyone to shorten it, stylise it how she wished, and Bethany could not argue.

They were soon approaching the end of the journey, turning onto a gravel path that was hardly wide enough to accommodate their car. Dad muttered that even a moped would have difficulty travelling this path, and mum just smiled. Tall trees hemmed each side of the road, and their wavering branches scratched at the roof of the car. Bethany could hear the branches tapping and scraping, while twigs swatted the windows. It was a rutted, narrow road, as if designed only for those who preferred to travel precariously.

The house came into view like a slide in a picture viewer. Aunt Jennifer had been left the picturesque four-bedroom home by their grandmother, who had thought the poor woman needed the security more than her son (who hadn't married anyone as indignant as Uncle Mick). The old woman had been right in that sense, but Bethany's dad was certain that Mick was only married to Jennifer for the sole reason of acquiring the property if and when his sister finally succumbed entirely to her husband.

The sound of the tyres catching the gravel broke the silence, sending perhaps every bird in every tree skyward. The day remained calm otherwise, and not a hint of cold was in the air.

"Bethany, can you grab the bags from the back seat?"

The young girl nodded and pulled free the bags that had been belted down. Closing the car door, Bethany walked to the front of the house where her cousin Stephen came to greet them.

"Aunt Linda! Uncle John!" the boy called, genuinely excited. He ran to his approaching relatives and gave each a tight hug. "And you, *Bee!*"

Another abbreviation, this one comical. She didn't mind; the boy was a year younger and not particularly bright for his age, but Bethany knew that his home life was often strained so she laid down the bags and squeezed him hard to let him know she was in good spirits, too.

"Little cousin!" she remarked. "Still ugly, like always!"

They laughed just as Aunt Jennifer appeared at the

doorway. Bethany's dad was the first to notice how unsightly she looked – whatever illness had taken hold was slowly and duly working its way through her. An illness associated with an unhappy marriage.

"Hello, John; Linda," she called, smiling at them. "It's so nice to see you all."

The frail woman stepped out of the house and threw her arms around her older brother; Bethany's dad, John, could feel the bones in his sister's back; *How thin she's getting*, he thought, scaring himself at the unsettling revelation.

The reunion was cut short by a smashing sound from inside the house. Aunt Jennifer jumped in her brother's arms, as if it had happened right next to her.

"That'll be Mick," she said hastily. "He's redecorating! He's upstairs–we'll leave him to it. Come, let's get you all inside."

The five of them left the warmth of the sunlight and slipped into the house that felt like time forgot.

THREE

BETHANY and Stephen sat in the living room drawing pictures with crayons as the adults prepared dinner in the kitchen. The kitchen was at the end of a long hallway; the house reminded Bethany of something out of Victorian times or like in one of those American prairie TV shows, where a busload of children grew up in a brooding hulk of a building only recently introduced to electricity and surviving on meagre food rations. There was a cultural feel to the place that Bethany associated with her late grandmother; nothing that alluded to usual perceptions that the homes of the elderly should be dim, floral-scented tragedies, but instead something that promoted warmth and brimmed with life and experience.

She could hear the adults talking, but ever so quietly, almost unperceptively; and above, Uncle Mick, methodically pacing around on the first floor, as he pasted and painted and papered the walls. Once or twice Bethany thought she heard a swear word or two rolling down the stairs; the insalubrious colour of Uncle Mick's language.

"Well?" Stephen asked, detaching her from her thoughts. "What have you drawn?"

"Um," she started, fumbling around on the floor at the spread of paper. "I sketched this: it's a fashion piece. Here we've got the head-dress and the robe, with the gold and... what?"

The young boy simply stared. He was unimpressed. The raised eyebrow told her so.

"You drew something better?" she asked, a little pointedly.

Stephen nodded.

"It's something that's real. I've seen it."

178

Bethany was intrigued. She held out her hand and he passed the paper over to her. Turning it the right way around, she recognised the playful attempt at blue sky, and the yellow sticks of corn or wheat or whatever it was that grew in the fields around the place. It was the form at the centre of the A4 sheet that held her attention: a green tent, unmistakable in its triangular shape. There was something immensely striking about its composition; although lacking any degree of photo realism or representation she was still certain that it was a tent. *A real wannabe Picasso!* she mused.

"It looks like a tent," Bethany said. "Just an ordinary green tent."

Stephen snatched the paper back.

"It's not ordinary! It's haunted."

"Haunted? How do you know?"

There was an odd look in the boy's eyes, something that indicated his statement was down to frightful suspicion and not acquired from any hard evidence, collected, and/or examined.

"I've been to see it with Kenny Smith and Danny Kay," Stephen explained. "We went there two weeks ago. The zip was down, but Kenny said he had been the day before and the zip was open!"

Bethany wasn't impressed.

"So?" Maybe it's some homeless person who lives in it? Or someone is camping. Doesn't mean it's haunted! That's just childish."

"I'm telling you, that tent is spooky, and it's *real*."

"Have you seen inside it?" she asked

"No, because it's haunted. There might be something evil living inside."

Just then, Aunt Jennifer made an appearance; and in some uncanny spousal synchronicity, Uncle Mick also appeared. But it was only she who stepped into the living room to be with the children.

"Are you alright, kids?" she asked them. "Dinner's almost ready."

"Thank God," Mick muttered. His face and hands were splattered with paint. "I've been up there all morning on my own. Whoever invented the bloody idea needs their head kicked."

Aunt Jennifer did her best to maintain the kids' attention, and away from the paint-splattered brute.

"Bethany, how is school? Your mum and dad said that you're doing well in art."

Bethany nodded to confirm.

"I like to draw, and so does my friend, Michelle. We do projects together that we often get certificates for."

Uncle Mick walked across the room.

"At least one child in this family has its head screwed on."

"Well, good for you, darling," Aunt Jennifer praised. "Is that your picture?" She was referring to the fashion piece. "Wow! Maybe one day you'll be designing clothes for the stars!"

Stephen raised his tent drawing.

"I drew this, mum."

Aunt Jennifer took the paper from him. She looked at it disapprovingly.

"That's not the horrible old thing by the railway bridge is it, Stephen? You stay away from that… that *tent*. It's dirty, and nobody knows what's inside. Could be anything. Or any*one*. Just stay away–do you understand?"

She returned his Picasso-in-practise and made to return to the kitchen.

"Dinner will be in ten minutes. Make sure your hands are washed, and then come through to the kitchen. We'll be sitting out in the back garden to enjoy the day."

As she left, she coughed so hard that it was as if something malicious had settled in her lungs and was refusing to let go.

FOUR

THE day out back was enjoyable, for their hard work preparing dinner was rewarded by a spot of sunshine that shone directly onto them. Even the winged insects stayed away long enough for them to eat and clear their meal, although the prying eyes of an interested squirrel or two hadn't escaped them. Aunt Jennifer sat with her brother and his wife at one side of the long wooden rectangular table; but Uncle Mick dined inside, chewing on his meal with apparent resentment as he stared at the group outside the window. Bethany's dad knew that their appearance today was likely to have fuelled any rage in Mick, but if the brute wanted to stir up any kind of trouble—verbal or physical—he would soon set him right.

"Eat up all of your bread," Aunt Jennifer urged her son. "It's good for you. Your Aunt Linda baked it herself."

The boy looked at both women, unaware just how much each wanted the world for their children. The design of a child, an implication of innocence.

"I will," he told them. "With this ham the bread tastes amazing!"

Bethany gulped down her lemonade. She was enjoying her food too and was really immersing herself in the environment in which her cousin lived. She thought how commonplace it was where she lived: there were nosey dogs instead of curious squirrels; gas-belching cars in place of carbon dioxide-drunk trees—even the cat-collecting old crone who lived across her street seemed as grumpy as Uncle Mick.

The delight of having her family visit was evident in Aunt Jennifer's eyes and in her smile; in every gesture the frail woman could display. Bethany sussed that there was nothing else in the world that the lady would prefer doing on a warm day like this than be surrounded by the people who genuinely loved and cared for her. It was healthy for her, for Stephen too, to be reminded that–while they resided like hermits–they were still very much a solid, welcome part of the family.

Stephen led Bethany to the swing that Uncle Mick had set up at the bottom of the garden. It was a rusting blue frame, but the ropes held taut and the seat was level and stable enough to hold either of them. Bethany sat on it first while Stephen pushed her gently.

"Have you given it any thought?" he asked from behind.

"About what?"

"The tent," he continued. "The haunted one."

"No, actually, I haven't. Why? You heard what your mum said, that you were to stay away from it."

Stephen pushed.

"I'm just saying, maybe we could investigate it–see what it's like inside."

Bethany scraped her shoes on the dirt beneath the seat to slow herself. She held onto the ropes as she turned to face him.

"Are you serious?"

Stephen nodded slowly, a grin forming more gradually.

"But what if we get caught? I mean, how far is the tent from here?"

A hopeful expression flitted across his young, chubby face.

"It's only about twenty or so minutes' away. It's beyond the back woods, past the trees where the old railway bridge is. And we wouldn't be gone long, so we wouldn't really be far from here."

Bethany chewed over the idea. She had to acknowledge some curiosity over the mysterious tent, but the possible dangers that may be lying in wait quelled that craving for knowledge. What if someone occupied it? Who would they be? And why was it there in the first place? All those questions suddenly increased the desire to know–a psychology that provided sustenance for a child's hunger to explore.

"I overheard dad saying to my mum that we should stay the night," Bethany told him. "I think he's worried about your mum. He wants to keep an eye on her. Do you think…?"

"What? That we should go *tonight*?" Stephen exclaimed.

"As long as we don't get too close, I think we could manage a little trip. What do you say?"

Grinning again, he began to push his big cousin.

FIVE

BY the time evening arrived the family had retreated into the house where, surprisingly, Uncle Mick had set a roaring fire in the living room. He didn't receive any thanks from his in-laws except for a hug from his wife who remarked on the homely, warm feel of the room. He basked in her gratefulness before disappearing upstairs.

There was a radio on the cabinet in the living room which Aunt Jennifer suggested that they listen to. Everyone gave a facial acknowledgement to the idea, nodding and smiling at her, and she switched it on and tweaked the dial until she found some soft music playing. There were no objections to her choice.

The adults sat on the couch while the two youngsters prepared themselves for bed. The time was going on 8 P.M. and weariness had settled upon the party, but Bethany and Stephen were hiding their energies.

"We're going upstairs now," said Stephen, approaching his mum. "I'll get the fold-out bed and make it up for Bee, okay? Good night, mum. Goodnight, Aunt Linda, Uncle John."

Aunt Jennifer kissed her son and thanked him. Bethany announced that she would help him make the bed. The children bade goodnight to their respective parents and together they walked up the stairs to Stephen's room, the twinkle in their eyes sparkling like jewels at the thought of their forthcoming adventure.

*****

The remainder of the evening was uneventful, and all four adults were sound asleep by 11 P.M. Uncle Mick was snoring soundly in his bed with his wife, while Bethany's parents slept on a futon downstairs.

The moonlight acted as a torchlight, thus enabling Bethany and Stephen to exit the bedroom without incident. They had redressed with each adding a jacket to their earlier attire, and, with one behind the other, Bethany led the youngster down the hallway to the top of the stairs. Their subsequent descent was flawless in its silent precision.

Tip-toeing through the living room, Stephen brushed past Bethany and opened a kitchen drawer.

"We'll need the back-door key," he whispered, carefully feeling around in the drawer with his hand. "To lock it outside, and then for when we get back."

Stephen closed the drawer softly and momentarily held up the key in triumph. He inserted it into the lock, turned it, and gently, with a devilish cunning opened the door just enough for them to squeeze through, before locking it again on the outside.

"Okay?" asked Bethany. "Lead the way."

They started off down the back garden—where again the moonlight acted as their guide—running now, past the large table, beyond the swings, and into the shadows of the bushes. They had woods the length of a football field to cover, with a time-length that Stephen had estimated to be around twenty minutes. They would manoeuvre their way through the woods, traverse the cornfields, and then cross the disused railway bridge to the location of the tent. But they found that negotiating fallen branches and muddy puddles wasn't easy in the dark. The moon was now glitter-balling its light through the tree canopy, bending and curving the bough-strewn duff and skewering their perspective of the land ahead.

They eventually reached the woodland's edge, a victory akin to a try or a touch-down back in the real world. Bethany thanked her younger cousin sarcastically for the excursion, as she itched herself from the ankles up. She was certain she had been bitten en masse by flying, nocturnal insects.

Stephen tried to perk her up.

"There's not far to go now, Bee," he assured her. "Once we make it through these cornfields, it's just the bridge to cross and then we're there."

Bethany sighed, accepting that it was she who planted the seeds of their trek anyway, and hurried him on. They had already been stumbling nearly fifteen minutes by the time they exited the woods. At least the cornfields were only, at worst, waist-high.

The first stalk whacked against her side and she fumed.

"How are *you* not getting hurt in this?" she said aloud, almost growling at him.

Stephen glanced back.

"Because I've done this before."

Bethany angrily swiped another stalk away. The bristling of swaying stalks sounded like a hundred brush-heads rubbing against one another around her. Their light was brighter now, the moon giving the fields a patina of silvery-gold shine and making everything around them much easier to see.

She stomped and kicked, flattened, and snapped much of the remaining way, while Stephen's lighter, more fleeting, body could breeze through. She could see his small frame ahead, pushing through the stalks with ease, darting this way and that; and she was also aware of a creeping *un*ease, something unsettling that was trying to consume them in this night maze. As if they were being watched from afar by eyes that could see everything. No, it was as if it was *she* that was being observed.

The rusting frame of the bridge appeared seconds after they both slipped out of the cornfields.

Stephen stood silently, his hands on his hips, resting. Bethany caught up and stood beside him.

"Remind me never to buy Cornflakes again!" Her light-hearted remark made the boy smile.

"We're about two minutes from the tent," he calmly informed her. "Can you feel it?"

Bethany shuddered. Quite suddenly the air was becoming cool, and the wind was picking up around them and whistling through the fields behind.

"Feel what?"

"Like there's something here," Stephen said, staring into the distance. "Watching us."

"Your mind's playing tricks on you! There's nothing to be afraid of. C'mon, we'd better move. We've spent too much time out here already."

Again, they started to march, this time on much smoother ground. The ground beneath them was dark-coloured and beat, but kind to their soles.

Fear was a funny thing when measured against curiosity; the balance between what we don't know and what we could know weighs heavy at both ends, but a decision must be reached and so fear, in this case, played a close second to their summoning courage and satisfying curiosity.

Stephen squatted, urging Bethany to do the same.

"What is it?" she whispered.

"Nothing, I just wanted to make sure that if there was someone there, we'd be out of their sight. When we go down over that ridge, the tent's in full view."

They duck-walked a couple of yards before sliding to the edge of the grassy ridge, their chins resting on the grass.

"Look over to the right," instructed Stephen. "You can't miss it."

Bethany brushed her hair from her face. The wind was starting to be annoying, but she had to see clearly. She shuffled forward and, like a meerkat, raised her head to peer over the ridge. Sure enough, down to the right, was the tent.

Unlike in the boy's crude drawing she had viewed earlier that day, here was the thing stark against the backdrop of a thick sky. Its dense and distinct form–pegged to the ground–never moved despite the wind blowing into it. It was like a solid prism encroaching into her frame of view.

"Does it look empty?" Bethany started, suddenly remembering Stephen by her side.

"It's hard to tell. Now, if someone *is* inside, they could be sleeping."

Stephen thought for a moment.

"What do we do?"

"We've seen it now, I believe you," she conceded. "I don't think we need to get any closer."

"But maybe we could check it a little, even just stay out here," he suggested.

Bethany remained staring at the tent. She couldn't tell if the front was closed or not.

"But I believe you that the tent's real," she said. "You win, okay?"

A sudden gust blew over them, and for the first time, Bethany saw the entrance flap open.

"It's not zipped down! It's not!" said Stephen, excitedly. If it wasn't for him lying down, he might've been jumping in the air.

"That does not mean we need to go in," Bethany told him.

"I'll go," Stephen said. "Just a bit, enough to see inside when the next wind blows. If there's anyone there, we're off. Okay?"

Bethany rolled her eyes.

"This could be dangerous," she said, the tone of her voice bordering on worry. "It could be someone who's a right crackpot, and then what do we do? Race through the fields like the Children of the Corn? No, thanks Stephen *King*, we need to get home."

He didn't listen to her; before she knew it, he was half standing and was about to approach the tent. She tried pulling him back, but her fingers slipped from his jacket.

"See you down there, *Bee!*"

Stephen crouched and made his way to the clearing where the tent was pitched. He kept to the one side, and, with the aid of some tall, prickly grass, remained unseen. Bethany watched him move like a character in a computer war game, with all the machismo and bravado of every ten-year old boy she had ever known.

Within a minute, he was close to the front of the tent. The

two of them kept their eyes fixed on it should any occupants decide to vacate it for a midnight toilet break, or whatever. Bethany supposed that since they had come all this way it would be a waste to go back with nothing learnt. Besides, maybe a quick glance into this marquee-home would put an end to the mystery. Yeah, that was it: she *would* get closer.

By the time Bethany made it to the tent, Stephen was already peeking in. The wind had blown the entrance open again and he saw that there was no body–shape, figure, or otherwise–in there. The thought hadn't occurred to them that as they had been spying on the tent, someone may have been spying on *them*.

"I can see *stuff*," said Stephen, holding the entrance flap open. "But there's definitely no-one in there."

Bethany crept closer.

"Doesn't look haunted, either. I think we can say that there's nothing to worry about here."

She felt an urge to move further in, to explore the innards of the tent. She could just make out papers and bottles, and something ragged that looked like a well-used sleeping bag. The silent night enveloped them; encouraging her too, to go in.

On her hands and knees, she slowly crawled forward. Her hands could feel the cold nylon of the groundsheet, and the prickly grass beneath. There were crumbs that pressed into her palms, which she wiped off hurriedly. Stephen remained on the outside, holding the flap open, keeping watch.

She felt the rubber handle of a small torch and after some probing, the switch. She looked back at Stephen, holding up the torch to show him. He looked in, nodding in acknowledgement.

She switched it on, and the inside of the tent lit up. In later years, Bethany would remember this moment as perhaps the main catalyst that disturbed and broke her mind; the one event that awoke the demon creature, Amy, alerting her of Bethany's plight. Had she not switched on the torch, the sordid remnants of an addict's haven would have remained unseen.

Pornography magazines appeared to be the favoured leisure pursuit here; Bethany unwittingly shone the circle of light over the glossy spreads of naked women of bygone eras; women with their big breasts hanging out, holding and displaying them wantonly for the viewer's pleasure. She gasped at the 'mystery' she had solved; at the gross treasure she had found. There were pictures of stocking-legged women exhibiting themselves alone; some with one or multiple male partners; others cavorting with women with tongues and fingers and various sex toys. In other magazines nearby there was more of the same, except one or two spreads featured women experimenting with all kinds of phallic objects.

The young girl felt sick to her stomach. She wanted to cry out, alert Stephen, but she couldn't let him see this filth. She dropped the torch and the light gleamed upon bottles of assorted colours and substances, some without labels but all recognisable as containers of beer. She doubted whether it was beer inside them, judging from the acrid smell they gave off.

She fumbled for the torch, close to tears and vomiting. She wished she hadn't turned the damn thing on. Gripping it she thumbed the switch back and killed the light. In the darkness, she could still see those naked parts, hanging and spreading–things being *inserted*.

She crouched past Stephen as she exited; he let go of the flap and watched her as she stood, shaking uncontrollably.

"You okay, Bethany? What was in there? What did you see?"

With much effort, Bethany tried to compose herself.

"Nothing. It was nothing, Stephen. Come, we need to go. We've been out long enough."

Stephen slowly got to his feet.

"You sure you're okay?"

Bethany grabbed hold of his hand.

"Stephen, *never, ever* come near this… *thing* again. Promise me that?"

The young boy simply looked on, perplexed and speechless.

"PROMISE ME!"

He buckled a bit as she reached out for his hand.

"Sure, Bee. Okay. Please, let go—you're hurting my hand! Hey, why are you crying?"

"From now on, you've no further business being here. *Listen to your mother.*"

She dragged him away and back onto the tracks that would return them back to the cornfields. They didn't speak a single word all the way home, but each knew there were a thousand things to say.

SIX

The next morning, after a vivid, horrendous succession of nightmares, Bethany tried to forget about the tent. She was still a young girl, still sensitive to the world, to pharmaceuticals being tested on animals, to baby chickens being slaughtered for the promise of fast food. She hadn't allowed herself to grow up but last night she had walked into something diabolical, something not fit for her. She saw magazine images of the boundaries of human contentment, though not wholly representative of; looked at consented degradation and glossy snapshots of acts that schools taught were only fit for love. It disturbed her, shook her inside, but what else did she expect to find? Was there a rainbow ending in the tent? Had she hoped it would lead to wherever had Alice went? It was a discovery that would now remain with her forever.

In the proceeding months, as more and more warnings of her impending doom were spelled out to her in various devilish-inspired ways, she would find out from Stephen that the tent was still there, though he had not returned to it, as per instructed.

In dreams for the next few years, up until her fifteenth birthday, she would sometimes see that swamp-green prism in the field; and behind her a train would speed by, and as it rolled along the tracks–across the bridge–its squeaks and rattles and hoots would mock her. She would dream that she was standing beside the tent, and the canvas entrance would be flapping in the wind, catcalling her to enter.

And in Hell, a creature would be sitting waiting patiently to begin the young girl's retribution.

BIO

Steven Deighan is a multi-internationally published, award-winning horror writer from Scotland. He is the author of the story collections *Things From The Past* (2006), *Stages of Undress* (2009), and *Submit Horror* (2019). He created the graphic book *Feels Like Stephen King* (2009) and the 3D comic book *The Party* (2015).

Steven is a stroke survivor who struggled with partial survivor's guilt (this stems from a successful recovery)—he harbours some emotional imbalance as a result. In 2019, he underwent heart transplant surgery on Easter Sunday at the Golden Jubilee National Hospital: the date Jesus was said to have risen from the dead.

Steven, in his thirties, feels just as resurrected. Although he privately embraces atheism, this is an irony that he contemplates daily.